Make Me Merry

A RETURN TO COAL HAVEN NOVELLA

MARIE JOHNSTON

LE PUBLISHING

Copyright © 2023 by Marie Johnston

Editing by Evident Ink

Proofing by MBE, Judy's Proofreading, and Deaton Author Services

Cover by Secret Identity Graphics

All rights reserved.

No part of this book may be reproduced in any form or by any electronic or mechanical means, including information storage and retrieval systems, without written permission from the author, except for the use of brief quotations in a book review.

The characters, places, and events in this story are fictional. Any similarities to real people, places, or events are coincidental and unintentional.

No AI Training

 Created with Vellum

Dear Santa,

All I want for Christmas is a quiet week on my mom's ranch while she's gone and to watch my nieces and nephews open presents on Christmas morning.

I'd also like to be rescued from a power outage in a snowstorm and be thrown into the warm bed of a hot man. Even better if I've had a major thing for that guy for most of my life. If I walk in on him doing laundry when every stitch of his clothing is in the wash, I'll consider that the best present ever.

What I'd really like for Christmas is for him to get over our age difference and the fact that he works for my mom and finally admit he has feelings for me. But that might be a Christmas miracle I won't receive.

Christmas wishes,

Nora Barron

One

NORA

"You're just going to hang out at the house all by yourself until Christmas?" Holden, my normally unflappable brother, frowned. He was wearing jeans and a heavy flannel. His hair was ruffled, but that could be more from the way his wife's hands had been all over him. They'd arrived on an impromptu date when I'd called to tell him I was in town for the next week.

Emery had peeled herself off him to talk to my cousin Isla, the owner of the brewery. I loved seeing my brother happy. Emery had become a sister, and between her kids and the boy she and my brother had together, I couldn't have asked for a better or bigger family.

Although tonight was the perfect example of being surrounded by people and feeling very much alone. Would I get what they had someday?

Maybe if I could quit comparing every guy to the one I had set on a pedestal years ago.

Maybe if other guys would stop falling so pathetically short.

The noise of the brewery had simmered to a dull roar. I'd been sitting at the bar for two hours, chatting with family members who'd stopped in and were surprised to see me in Coal Haven for the Christmas holiday.

I didn't live far away, but I missed home. Bismarck was small for a city, but even the cozy town was much larger than my hometown. My mom had left for one of her sporadic beach vacations with some man she'd just met. A habit that had resulted in both my older brother and me. Different dads, same impulsive idea that Mom could play nice with someone before her toxic personality corroded everything.

I loved my mom, but as a pair, we were complicated. She thought she birthed her opposite when I was growing up and resented me for it. I pretended her attitude didn't bother me, which irritated the hell out of her more.

"That's the plan," I said, nursing the water I had switched to after the hard apple cider Isla had made from apple trees on my mom's land. She'd been so excited to get the license needed to make hard cider. Her dad, my uncle, had probably ordered my mom to share the apples she never used.

Holden's brow furrowed. "You know about the winter storm that's supposed to hit early tomorrow morning, right?"

The crowd in the brewery was thinning out, likely due to that storm. The snow was supposed to start nice and heavy for a day or two before the wind picked up. It would be the second big one of the year, and Christmas was next weekend.

"Yes, *Dad*," I said sarcastically.

He'd been more of a father figure than a brother thanks

to Mom's commitment-phobe ways. Mom would've let me go feral if it hadn't been for Holden. I wasn't a boy, and she didn't know, or care, about what to do with me. Holden hadn't fared much better, honestly.

"That's why I came early," I said. I vaguely gestured toward the windows. "Which is why I said I'd do the chores while I'm here. You can hunker down with your family and not worry."

"By yourself?" he repeated.

I sighed. Holden worried. I should be touched, but the insult burrowed into my conscience. "You don't think I can handle it."

"It's not that, Nora. It's a storm. I'd be concerned about any of my relatives out there alone. Usually Mom has Colt, but he's...doing whatever it is he does when he goes away."

My interest naturally perked up at the mention of Colt. The yearning and desire I'd gotten used to ignoring flared back to life. Pointless feelings for a man I'd known almost half my life. A man who was still a big mystery. Colt Jensen.

A handsome, bearded mystery who spoke in little more than grunts and curt commands around me. He'd been hired by Mom when I was a kid. I had assumed he was just another guy she'd run around with before killing any affection he harbored for her. But that hadn't happened. Colt stayed and worked. He and Mom maintained a firm work relationship, neither showing a single bit of more than professional interest in each other, and the rest of us guessed at his age. I thought he was a little older than Holden, who was approaching forty.

I thought a lot when it came to Colt.

Colt had ignored me when I was a kid. When I went to college and came back, he'd look at me like I was an alien who'd walked off a spaceship and didn't know how the world worked. As I got older, he'd distanced himself more.

Five years ago, I finally admitted to myself that I was head over boots for a guy who'd rather not acknowledge my existence.

He'd apparently taken his lead from my mother.

"You wouldn't worry about Colt," I muttered. How many times had Colt worked the ranch while Mom shacked up with a guy for a weekend or went away for ten days like she was doing now? A lot. Unusual to have them both gone. Colt wouldn't be back until after Christmas, leaving before even Mom had. She might know where he went on his time off, but he didn't tell anyone else.

"I would, and I would tell him I was worried about him just to make him cranky."

I chuckled. Holden would do, and probably had done, exactly that. "I promise I'll call if I run into any trouble. This is my vacation, though, and I'm looking forward to playing in the snow." Even if that snow was pelting me at fifty miles an hour.

"Your coffee shop runs on its own with no problems while you're away?"

"There are never no problems." Doubt about the biggest adventure in my life would always be present, but I was proud of the place and had some excellent employees. "But I have a good manager, and I baked ahead."

"Did you bring any treats with you?"

I smiled at the caution in his tone. My "treats" were notoriously unpopular with my family. They didn't appreciate gluten-free brownies. Macarons with real fruit for color and natural flavors fell flat on their taste buds. And my sugar substitutes had been gagged on for far too long. As my brother, Holden had tried to be as supportive as possible, and I appreciated it. He didn't run from my desserts like our cousins did, but he also didn't enjoy them. "No, I'm not subjecting you to the torture of organic and natural ingredients."

He grunted. "It's fine. Your stuff is good."

My stuff was good, but not to him. "I found my audience, and none of them have the last name Barron."

"I'm not shocked. Business is booming though?"

I could've joined Mom on vacation from my smoothie sales alone, but I hated to be boastful. "Business is going well. I've contracted with local producers—growers, bakers, chefs—and that's taken the time burden off of me."

"You invested your trust fund money well." His gaze scanned the brewery built in the old train foundry and repair shop. "Both you and Isla."

Isla and I had started businesses with the old oil money left to us by our grandparents. My brother and Isla's brother had both built homes. All of us secured a future independent from our parents.

"When are you going to open a second place? Hit up a new town, become a franchise?" His eyes crinkled at the corners, but his teasing wasn't mean spirited.

"I don't think I'm ready." Normally, I loved to talk about work, but the natural caution I had around my family extended to my brother. He was supportive, but he butted into my business as much as the next family member, and I didn't want to talk about how expanding terrified me. Opening a coffee shop with a large trust fund was one thing. But that money was sunk into Bean Good. Doing it again meant I had to be a savvy entrepreneur.

"So, are you going to let me do chores for you and shovel out after the storm?" I went for a subject change. I was no longer the sickly sister he had to watch out for, and I could help him this time.

He gave me a dubious look as Emery slid into his side.

He shifted to fit her between his legs and hugged her to him. Sweet.

God, I wanted to be that close to someone—and have him be a decent guy. Definitely not a guy who couldn't quit talking about how much he had in Bitcoin while asking if I could get the check to our date night "this one time." It'd been every time.

Holden whispered loud enough for me to hear in Emery's ear, "Nora thinks I'm going to sit back and let her dig Mom's house out by herself."

Emery's mouth quirked. She wore a dark gray hoodie I remembered Holden wearing. She might've commandeered it, but I doubted there was one thing he didn't give her if she wanted it. "He might be afraid to let you use the new tractor with the snowblower attachment your mom is so proud of."

I snickered. Mom had almost no faith in me, and the lack stretched to equipment I'd grown up around and had often used. "Back into a farm truck once…"

"Twice," Holden said.

"And how many fences have you run over moving snow?"

He grinned. "Five more than Mom knows about."

Laughing, I pushed away from the bar. "I'll put my presents to the kids in your pickup in case the storm lasts longer than we think."

"We're leaving too. You got everything you need at the house?" He helped Emery get her coat on. She smiled at him. He'd probably done it a thousand times since they met, but she still said thank you and looked at him like he was a hero.

Longing tugged at my heart. Seeing them made me feel oddly better about my dismal dating life. I wasn't settling until I had what they had. "I picked up groceries in Bismarck before I left town and unloaded them already." I'd safely tucked the food away and stashed my luggage in my old room. "The freezer's full of meat."

"Mom never checks the main generator, but Colt runs his periodically. If the power goes out and the generator craps out, you can seek refuge in his place."

Shivers traced down my spine. Colt's place. The forbidden zone for the mysterious man. Since he'd arrived, he'd been staying in a mother-in-law suite built into the newest shop. Colt had never let me into his quarters. Looking back, I could see why an adult man wouldn't let a nosy teen into his place. According to the talk of the town, which I had listened to with wide-open ears when it came to Colt, he also never brought his random hookups there either. I doubted anything had changed since I'd moved five years ago. He was an intensely private guy.

Small consolation, but it'd made me feel better for years. I spent way too much time wondering if he was as good as the gossip said he was. I'd also spent way too much time seething with jealousy. Envy-green wasn't my color, and Colt wasn't going to be my man. Ever.

I gave Holden and Emery a hug and drove to Mom's house. I parked in her empty stall in the detached garage. Outside, clouds clogged the sky, and the fresh smell of impending snow was in the air. Cozy nights with a book sounded divine after the rat race of building the coffee shop, waking up early every morning baking and brewing and covering shifts until I had a well-trained, reliable staff.

I reached the side door that was between the house and the garage. Mom was too stubborn to build a breezeway to protect the space from the elements. Said it'd make her weak. Instead, it was just another area I'd have to shovel when the storm was done. And because of the way the wind blew, the drifts could be over six feet high. But I'd do it just so Holden could tell Mom I did all the work.

We'd both enjoy that.

Warm air surrounded me when I walked into the mudroom off the kitchen. I toed off my shoes and paused. Why was it so comfortable and not frigid? Mom had cranked the thermostat down while she was gone, and I hadn't turned it up when I stopped in earlier.

A light I hadn't noticed was on shone from the living room. Were other family members stopping in to check on things? A tiny spark of fear ignited. Was it family? Did someone think they were going to squat in the house while Mom was gone and walk right in thinking the place would be empty?

Dammit, if I got stabbed for being oblivious there was an intruder not bothering to hide, Holden would never let me forget it. Mom would be like a terrier with a precious toy. She wouldn't let it go.

Should I call out? Give my intruder an alert I was home?

I put my keys between my fingers and crept forward. How effective was the whole key thing anyway? I envisioned hurting myself more. I was tough, but that was like "stay on a spooked horse" tough. Not "fight off an unknown intruder who probably had loads more muscle than me" tough.

Still, I wasn't leaving. If it was Uncle Cameron checking on the house, he'd get cranky about me calling the cops, and I just wanted to avoid family drama.

Spinning into the kitchen, my gaze landed on a spectacular bare ass standing in front of the open fridge door. The flexed mounds dimpled in on each side. Wide, muscled shoulders were flexed as strong arms gripped either side of the fridge. Dark tattoos spotted with red—playing cards— covered his shoulder blades and wound down his arms. A horse head was in the middle of his back. A strangled gasp left my mouth, and the man turned to look over his impressive shoulder.

Oh.

My.

God.

Colt. I'd never seen Colt bare more than his face and arms in my entire life. He didn't wear shorts. He didn't work without a shirt—at least not when I could see. His trimmed beard hid half his face.

The beard part was still true. But the rest? Not one stitch of clothing.

"Fuck," he barked and fully spun around, his horrified gaze on me.

Air was suctioned out of my lungs in a long wheeze.

All the rumors were true. They had to be with that beast between his legs. Heavy and thick and…I'd never admired a ball sack before, but his said, "Look at me and be in awe."

He slapped a hand over his privates, but let's be honest. That wasn't enough. I cocked a brow.

"Quit looking, Nora," he growled.

I coughed out a laugh, not even ashamed at being caught staring. "I can't. You have a lot to look at." A manic giggle left me. I had barely noticed the erratic skulls etched into his pecs or the barbed wire running along his collarbone. I'd known he had tattoos, but I'd had no idea his torso was covered. Or that he had a spiderweb on one thigh with a black widow in the middle.

"Christ, girl. You're going to kill me." He sidestepped, and the fridge door shut, smacking his ass on the way.

My giggles got higher in pitch, and he stopped to glare.

I couldn't contain myself. The shock. The impressive sight. Seeing Colt actually flustered. I doubled over, laughter erupting from me.

He whipped a dish towel out of a drawer and flicked it

open with a crack. "Women don't usually break down laughing when they see my junk."

"That is not junk," I said through peals of laughter. "That is why dicks were historically broken off statues. Women couldn't control their reactions."

He made a choked sound. "I doubt that's true."

I straightened, wiping the corners of my eyes. Heat flooded my body despite the laughter, but Colt was still firmly outside his box, and that helped me forget he was naked in the same room as me. "It might be. The history books aren't going to say 'And therefore, Caesar McGuilicuddy was jealous of his wife's fascination and took a hammer to the marble phallus.'"

He blinked at me. Blinked again. The towel covered his cock, unfortunately, but the rest of his body was on display. Flames worked their way up my face.

I'd walked in on him naked. What was he doing nude—

No. Not while I was in this house. If he'd started bringing women home, he'd have to pause until the new year. "If you brought one of your hussies here to fuck around while Mom's gone, you'd better keep the sex fest in your own place. I'm staying until after Christmas." The burn inside me was no longer from stark feminine appreciation.

Jealousy blazed through my veins.

He jutted his chin out like he was trying to hear better. "Hussy?" Unless he backed out of the room, there was no way for him to retreat without me getting a full moon. And hey, if he was content to catch up with nothing but a dish towel covering that impressive cock, I was more than okay with an eyeful of abs.

"Yes. I'm sure she's a nice girl, but I don't want her fucking you in my mom's house while I'm here." I didn't want her fucking him regardless, but I couldn't exactly admit that.

His gaze intensified. He was centering himself, gathering in and closing his emotions off. This was the first time I'd witnessed him doing it. The door to what he was thinking or feeling was usually firmly shut. "I'm not fucking anyone tonight." He said it almost as if he was trying to convince himself.

"You don't have company?" Then what was he doing? Shock and jealousy were giving way to confusion.

He shook his head and glanced down at himself. A sheepish expression flitted over his face, and I was riveted. I was seeing more of Colt than ever—nudity aside. "The washing machine in the shop is busted. I didn't know you were here—I thought the house was empty."

"I thought you were gone."

"I came home early to beat the storm. Didn't want Holden worrying about this place when he has a wife and kids at home."

This. This was why I couldn't get over Colt and why every guy I'd tried to fall hard for couldn't compare. Consideration was built into him. He just took care of what needed taking care of, didn't matter if it was the cattle, the house, the property, or my car. He got it done, and he didn't complain.

But I wasn't going to sit around while he worked. I wanted to relax, but I also missed normal country life. A lot. "I told Holden I'd take care of it."

"I can do it. I'm home now."

"Why are you back already?"

Usually when I asked probing personal questions, he turned away or changed the subject. I resigned myself to getting no answer.

He worked his mouth. "I wasn't...needed."

Oh. I tilted my head, unprepared for an actual response. The vagueness wasn't a surprise, but the raw honesty was. "I'm sorry you felt that way."

He lifted a burly shoulder. The tattooed barbed wire rippled. I stroked my gaze over his broad chest. Dark hair scattered over his defined pecs and trailed down his abdomen. The same dark hair dusted his legs. How would they feel to curl up to at night?

What would it feel like to slide over his body from head to toe?

"Nora."

I jerked my gaze back up to his face.

He cleared his throat and shifted like he was nervous, only solid, strong Colt never got nervous and never around me. "Can you turn around until I find something to cover myself with? Something might be done in the dryer."

The laundry room was on the other side of the kitchen. He made a circle in the air with his finger.

"Oh. Sorry." I spun around.

I couldn't summon one ounce of apology. If other guys hadn't been able to live up to Colt before I'd seen him naked, they didn't have a snowflake's chance in a bonfire now.

I waited, staring at the entry I'd come in from. A few flakes falling from the sky were visible through the window in the door. He must've arrived shortly after I stopped in at the brewery. "Didn't you notice the fridge was full of food?"

"I wondered why Kira left so much produce to spoil. Or why she had fruit at all."

"I can go to my room until you're done," I called.

"It's all right," came his muffled reply. "I've got one more load to dry, but my sweats are done."

I tapped my foot, replaying his fine, ink-free ass. Did he

do any other workouts besides ranch work to hone those muscles? Was it genetic?

"You can turn around," he said gruffly.

I did as he said. The flush returned, swamping my body. He was dressed, but I wasn't left disappointed. Gray sweats hung from his hips, showing his heavily muscled thighs better than his jeans did. The plain white shirt he wore was painted on his chest. "I'm almost more surprised to see you in sweats than to see you naked."

A faint pink dusted across his cheeks.

Oh.

My.

God.

"Are you blushing?" I blurted.

He scowled, but the flush deepened. "I don't blush."

"You do. You are."

"Nora."

He used to be able to quiet me with nothing more than my name in his deep voice. But the power balance between us had shifted. He was no longer a muscled god who left me flustered and wanting—and feeling utterly lacking because of his blatant disinterest. I was the one flustering him this time.

"It's okay to be human, Colt." I stuffed my keys into my jeans pocket and went to the fridge. He narrowed his eyes at me but didn't say anything. The line across his brow deepened. Was he bothered by my response? "Were you looking for something to eat? I can whip up a meal or find a snack."

"You don't have to cook for me." He wasn't reassuring. He sounded like my cousins when they asked if I was bringing something homemade to a family gathering. Nervous.

I stopped with my hand on the fridge handle and rolled

my eyes. "It'll be meat and potatoes, I promise. I was going to make myself a bite in case the house loses power."

He tried to hide his relief and failed. "Did Kira check the generator before she left?"

I shrugged and dug into the fridge, gathering the butter and ground beef. I hadn't planned to eat before bed, but my stomach rumbled, reminding me I hadn't had more than a piece of quiche at the coffee shop before I left Bismarck. "I didn't ask. She doesn't know I'm here."

He grunted. "Probably for the best."

One thing about Colt, he understood Mom, and he'd witnessed for years what things were like between me and her. "Hamburger?"

He eyed the pound of meat in my hand. It was still frozen. I couldn't commit the sin of buying ground beef when the freezer was full of processed Barron beef. I had taken a chub of beef out when I unloaded groceries.

"What kind of bun?" he asked warily.

I almost sighed. Colt wasn't as avoidant of my food as the rest of my family, but he wasn't a fan. "I'm sure Mom has a regular bun around here, or maybe there's some in the deep freeze. All I packed are gluten-free buns."

"Isla made a special batch of hard cider for you."

Had the gluten-free made him think of cider? "I had some tonight. She's always been supportive of me and my dietary issues."

"Kira doesn't get shit like that."

"Anything she doesn't want to deal with is all in my head." I was sick for a long time before I went to college and could actually go to the doctor without her permission or without her finding out I was "whining" again. I'd had ulcerative colitis and a lot of food sensitivities. I'd cleaned out my diet and diligently added food back to test what I could tolerate. My gut healed, and as long as I was careful, I was symptom-free.

And I made what I had learned my career.

Mom still thought I'd faked all my issues for attention.

"I'll try one of your gluten-free buns," he finally said. "Gotta be improved by now."

"Yes, they've come a long way. And I didn't bake these." I waved at the table, brushing my gaze over his broad chest one more time. "Have a seat, and let me cook for you."

His stare intensified. A muscle clenched in his jaw, then he padded barefoot to the little table Mom had her coffee and toast at every morning.

* * *

Colt

I lay in my bed and stared at my ceiling with my hands folded behind my head. My obnoxious erection was out and proud and annoying as fuck. My dick thought it was a good idea—an excellent one—to go back in the house and follow up on that impressed and appreciative expression Nora had when she saw me naked.

How could I not have noticed she was home?

Home. *That house isn't her home, fucker.* Nora didn't live in Coal Haven anymore. The years after she'd finished college and lived on the ranch had been a sheer form of torture for me.

Annoying little-kid Nora I could ignore. I'd spent my whole life ignoring kids—wasn't that why I returned early? Nora had been nothing but the sullen daughter of my employer. She'd had bad skin and a sallow appearance back then, but it hadn't mattered. She could've been a budding supermodel. I wasn't that guy.

When she'd come home for the summers during college, she was still pouty, and her catty arguments with Kira drove me crazy. At the same time, I'd admired her. Not many people could stand up to caustic Kira Barron, but Nora went toe-to-toe with her. She didn't just grit through a confrontation; she would happily engage in the same passive-aggressive shit Kira did. My boss got a taste of her own medicine with her daughter.

I'd felt guilty as hell when I heard Nora tell Holden about all her stomach issues. No wonder she hadn't been feeling well. It wouldn't have mattered if she'd been diagnosed while she lived at home. Kira would've force-fed the girl bread to toughen her up.

But then Nora had graduated from college and moved home, irritating her mother to no end.

And I'd noticed how Nora's skin glowed. How her cornflower-blue eyes twinkled when she laughed. The way her breasts pushed against her shirts and how her hips swayed when she walked.

I'd *noticed*.

I couldn't risk this job. I had no resume for future employers, and no one would want to hire a guy who'd been canned from one of the biggest ranching families in the area.

And I didn't do relationships. I wasn't fucking my boss's daughter either.

She'd seen me naked.

With a growl, I pushed out of bed. I still had on the sweats and shirt I put on from the dryer. I was in my room in the shop, and Nora was in the house, but I was hyper paranoid I'd give her another show, like I'd turn around and she'd be at my door.

Not that it seemed like she minded.

I went to the window and peered out. A curtain of wet, heavy snow fell. There was no wind, but the weight of the wet snow might be enough to tamper with the finicky power around here.

I stuffed my feet into my boots and went through the shop to outside and stopped. "What the fuck?"

Nora was stomping around in the snow, a wide smile on her face. She was in a puffy blue-and-white winter coat, a stocking hat with a bouncing tuft on the top, and thick boots that went to her knees. Snow dotted her back and knees like she'd fallen, waved her arms and legs, and got up to admire her snow angel.

Last I checked, it was after midnight. I hadn't expected a frolicking snow angel. She should be tucked in a warm bed, far away, where she couldn't haunt my dreams.

She stopped. "You're still awake?"

"Yes, I'm still awake. Why are you outside in the middle of the night in the dead of winter?"

She ticked her gloved finger up. "Technically, winter starts on the winter solstice, so it's still autumn."

"Tell that to Mother Nature."

She laughed, the tinkling sound quieting faster in the falling snow. "It's fun. I can't do this in town."

I stalked farther into the yard. She knew very well a storm was on its way. Now that she was here and I was here, I couldn't escape a sense of responsibility when it came to her safety. I didn't want to. Snowflakes pelted my cheeks and the top of my head. "You couldn't wait until morning?"

"The wind is supposed to pick up." She spun and lifted her face to the sky. Stopping, she sighed, a happy sound that went straight to my goddamn gut, making me have all kinds of thoughts about coaxing that noise from her again. "Besides, I had a coffee before I left town. I wasn't sure how long I was going to be up tonight, but..."

I waited for her to finish, but she dropped her arms, the joyous expression gone. I'd give anything to have it back. "But what?"

"But the quiet was harder to adjust to than I thought." When she glanced at me, she frowned. "Colt, go back inside. You're in nothing but a T-shirt."

Is that more than you want to see me in, snow angel?

I drop-kicked that thought out of my head. "I'll go inside when you go inside."

She pursed her lips and gave me a *really?* look. "I'm an adult, Colt."

Lots of adults died in snowstorms, and I couldn't bear to see one inch of her satiny skin frostbitten. "I've noticed, snow angel."

She drew back, her eyes widening. She shook her head. "Snow angel?"

I waved a hand out like I was irritated when I was really damn embarrassed the endearment slipped out. "What do you call that?"

"Frolicking."

I'd had the same thought. *Didn't mean a thing, dumbass.* "Isn't that what snow angels do?"

Her mouth quirked, and not for the first time tonight, I was drawn to those pretty pink, plump lips. Images flashed through my head—inappropriate. X-rated. I was way too old to be picturing her mouth around my cock. I'd known her far too long to have thoughts like that about her, but here I was. I embraced the frigid temp to keep my blood away from my groin. "Go inside so I can quit worrying about you."

She clapped her hands together, and snow puffed off. Flakes stuck to her stocking hat, her eyelashes, and gathered on her shoulders. She resembled a snow angel more and more. "You can quit worrying about me now, old man."

A frustrated noise gusted out of me. My beard was crusting, and I probably resembled Old Saint Nick. "How old do you think I am?"

She tiptoed through the snow, leaving perfect tracks that she turned around and inspected. I brushed snow off my head and shoulders and was only awarded with more.

"Hmm," she said, making another noise that went straight to my dick. "I think you're older than Holden."

I was aware my age, and any other facts about my life, were a topic of much speculation. If I started giving out details, more information would get uncovered, and there was plenty I wanted to stay buried. I didn't give a fuck about my age beyond that I was too old for Nora Barron.

Although she'd turned thirty. Our age difference wasn't—

Not yours, you geriatric fucker. "I'm forty-four."

"Oh." Her mouth formed a perfect O, and Christ, what I could do with that. "I didn't think you were that old."

Jesus. "I'm gonna go finish my AARP application and go to bed. Go inside, Nora."

"You can join younger than fifty, you know. For real."

I closed my eyes. Tonight was supposed to be a night I could re-center myself after remembering all the shit I should've done better and all the people I let down. It wasn't for Nora to remind me of the reasons why going after her would be fucked up.

Her giggles made me open my eyes. "What?" I bit out.

"I thought you liked the mystery. I didn't think you were sensitive about your age." She cleared her throat, suddenly serious. "Sorry, I wouldn't have teased you."

"I'm not sensitive about my age." Unless it came to her. "But I'm fucking cold. Go in."

"You go in."

A gust of wind snaked around the house and slapped

snow into my face. "Fuck. Goddammit. The wind's picking up. Go inside."

"Colt, the buildings are too close together to make it a whiteout. I can see the house just fine. I get that you're worried, and I'm touched, but I'm seriously enjoying myself."

I clenched my hands. They were going numb. Cold seeped into my skin, and my shirt was damp from the snow melting into it and more piling on. I could not go inside, get a coat, or hell, just stay in and relax while she was outside when the weather was getting shittier. But I couldn't bring myself to leave her for a second, like if I ducked inside, she'd blow away. "Go in, or I'll carry your ass in."

She held her arms out, her expression challenging. "Do it."

"Game on, snow angel." I needed the reprieve, and I needed to move to warm up. The energy coursing through me was hot. Anticipatory.

I stalked toward her.

She let out a squeal and darted to the side, but I was quicker. My boots slipped in the snow, but I'd tagged too many calves in my life in all sorts of weather to let that slow me down. I wrapped my arms around her waist, the cold fabric of her coat crinkling. I swooped her feet off the ground and marched toward the house.

I liked the weight of her in my arms way too much.

She laughed and shouted. "Colt!" More laughter.

My lips twitched. I had the strongest urge to join her laughing. I wasn't that guy either. I didn't do snowball fights or chase girls in some elementary school show of power. A girl wanted to fuck, we fucked. If she wasn't interested, I couldn't care less. Nora was on a different level. She affected me in a way that made me wonder if I couldn't have more. Then I'd remember I didn't deserve more.

"I can't believe you're doing this." She pushed at my chest, but she wasn't going anywhere.

"Believe it." I reached the side door and opened it. I didn't enter. The place was cozy, too inviting, especially with the owner away and the savory scents of Nora's excellent meal lingering in the air.

I wasn't a fan of her desserts, but she could handle my meat and potatoes any day.

Mind outta the gutter, pervert. I lowered her, but her winter clothing and the snow that had collected on her ended up sliding down my body and right over my dick. The thing didn't care that I was cold, wet, horny, and irritated. Nora was in my arms.

She turned as her feet hit the floor. Our faces were inches apart, and I couldn't move, too scared I'd do something I couldn't take back. I was an employee. That was it.

"Colt?" Her warm breath puffed out, and I leaned in. Minty. Would she taste the same?

I was so close. So many questions would be answered. Did her lips feel as soft and pillowy as they looked? Did she kiss as passionately as I suspected? Had a man kissed her properly—until her knees were rubber and her panties were soaked?

I lost the fight against my erection.

I jerked back. I couldn't torch what I had. I couldn't go back to being the guy I was. This was my second chance, and I'd dedicated my life to keeping it. "Stay inside." I slammed the door shut and stomped off.

Two

NORA

"Stay inside," I muttered in a deep voice that mimicked Colt's for the hundredth time today. "*Stay inside.*"

Why couldn't he have left me alone last night? Why did he have to be so grumpy and worried? The snow had been heavy but not storm-level bad.

On top of not being able to sleep after seeing him one, naked, two, in gray sweats, and three, being pressed against his incredibly hard body, I'd slept in. By the time I woke and rushed outside, he'd already fed and watered the horses, fed the cows, and checked their water, and the cats lazed around the barn like it was a summer day. Colt had given them the good food, the canned stuff he claimed stuck to their little ribs during cold weather.

Colt was a softie but hard in the best ways.

Too bad I was so irritated with him. He'd shoveled the path by the back door and cleaned out a drift behind the stall of the garage I was parked in. The drift had reformed and didn't that make me feel like Colt had shown off by going the extra mile while I snoozed.

Wind bucked snow into my face and stole my breath. Instead of the wet, heavy flakes from last night that absorbed the sounds of nature and made the ranch a magical place, today's snow was hard and small and vicious. This was a winter storm.

I hugged my coat tighter to myself. I'd stuffed a hat on my head and wore gloves, but maybe I should've put my snow pants on. A short stretch across the broad expanse of the driveway between the house and shop was open enough to befuddle the senses.

I plowed through to the shop and fought the door against the wind. Inside, I was stomping snow off my boots when I heard, "What's wrong?"

I glanced through the dim shop, lit only by the side windows, to the back. Colt was in jeans with a black shirt on under an untucked green flannel. He was on the mat in front of his door, like he'd stepped out as soon as he heard the shop door open.

He looked good. Like my old Colt again. Not *old*, but the Colt I knew.

Did our age difference bother him?

He'd have to find me more than a kiddish annoyance to think like that.

"I can't find the Christmas tree." I took my gloves off and sniffed, my nose slowly thawing out. I would spend Christmas Day, weather willing, with Holden and his family, but I could put up the tree, the one we'd celebrated around as kids. He'd always done his best to make the day special for me when Mom would rather head to the beach with some guy.

"She had me take it to the dump last year."

A small gasp left me. Last year? I'd asked her if I could

have the tree. The same tree as when I was a kid. The thing was ratty and ragged and canted to the left, but Holden had steadfastly put it up every year I was home.

"She did what?" The menace in my voice shocked me. How could she? She knew I'd loved that damn tree, and she'd turned around and had him throw it away. She hadn't even told me. To her, trashing the tree was a task. She hadn't even been concerned enough to taunt me with it. Like what I had said meant nothing.

"Threw it. Said it was no good." He stroked his gaze over my face. I didn't know what he saw, but his eyes filled with sympathy. "I didn't realize you were attached to it."

I curled my hands into fists, but I couldn't stop tears from springing into my eyes. It was Mom's job to know I was attached to it. Her job to care. I was an adult, but her slights continued to puncture my heart like a million tiny arrows. "Why, Colt? Why does she hate me so much? I've been asking for that damn tree for years, and she kept putting me off. 'When you get your own place. When you get a bigger place. Next year.'" I flung my arms up, my gloves flapping in my right hand. "She fucking threw it?"

Shaking my head, I spun, struggling to keep control. I couldn't break down in front of him. He'd think I was immature. Too young for him, thanks to my childish tantrum.

I sniffled again, only this time it had nothing to do with the weather. "I don't know what I did other than being born. She didn't like me sick and miserable, but she doesn't like me healthy and strong." I blinked rapidly, but the tears kept gathering. I couldn't turn around and face him. I should leave, but he understood, and I had no one else to talk to. "Thanks for telling me."

I'd skip decorating for the year. Put this holiday down as the most boring ever. Better than finding out she'd also trashed all the other decorations, which I hadn't found in my search.

I put my hand on the doorknob, bracing myself to face the wind, when he said, "She's jealous."

Mom was too hard to be jealous. "I doubt that."

"You have an older brother who dotes on you for one."

Her older brother definitely did not. My uncle Cameron, Isla and Stetson's dad, was the oldest. He had ruled with an iron fist. But while he was softening, my mom seemed to be growing more brittle. With me anyway.

"And you are strong and healthy," Colt continued. "You did that despite her. She'll say she doesn't believe in that food-sensitive bullshit and that ulcers—ulcerative collect— whatever the fuck you have—is a catchphrase in the social media world, but she doesn't like that she was wrong and you were right. You were sick, and she told you it was in your head."

I dropped my hand off the doorknob. I could understand what he was saying, but if that was the case, her treatment of me was even more depressing. "She's the parent. She needs to get over it."

"That's the other problem."

Slowly, I pivoted to face him. He was standing, looking all mountain-man hearty, concern in his eyes. I must look wan. Drawn. But it didn't matter. That emotion he was giving me a glimpse of told me I had to hear what he had to say.

"You intimidate her."

I laughed. "I do not." The idea was absurd.

He nodded, his gaze solemn. "I know you think your mom's tough as nails and twice as brash, but think about it. Her age. Her gender. Her job. Her family. She's been fighting an uphill battle from the beginning. People push her around, and she's had to fight for what she's got. But you fight her for what you've got, and you win. Even worse, you have family and friends who support you. Family she didn't have helping her."

"They weren't born yet." My cousins and I were forged by the fire of our parents, and we stuck together because of it. My cousins were more like siblings.

"Your mom's not immune to envy, Nora. Not even toward her own daughter."

When he said it like that...

"Doesn't justify her shitting on you," he finished roughly.

His words wrapped around me like a warm blanket. Someone else could see how she acted. Even more, he understood it. He shifted the conflict in my head. My mom's treatment was due to her personality, which I'd known. But she acted the way she did because of her, not because there was something about me that drove her to it. The focus wasn't that much different, but it was enough to give me something to think about during the storm.

"Thank you."

He lifted his chin in acknowledgment.

Had I been coming from such a defensive place I lacked empathy for my mother? We were both too alike in that sense. I could get over myself a little too. "And thanks for doing chores." I flashed him a sheepish smile. "Too much frolicking. I slept in."

His gaze darkened. "I'd better not find you out there again tonight."

Normally, I'd make a point of being rebellious, but it was storming out, and I wouldn't prove anything by being an idiot. "It's not snow angel weather."

"Nope." He went to the door of his apartment. "Text me when you get back to the house."

* * *

Colt

The cold was what woke me. I liked sleeping in arctic temps, but I'd kicked off my blanket and my balls were icy. My first thoughts turned to Nora. Did I wake because she was playing outside in the middle of the night again, and I couldn't miss it?

All in the name of making sure she was safe.

Blinking my eyes open, I blinked again. Fuck, it was dark. The wind raged outside, and other than that, my apartment was quiet. The fridge wasn't running. The fan of the furnace wasn't going. The power was out.

"Fuck. Nora." I needed to get the generator going. The farmhouse was old yet would hold heat better than a giant shop with minimal insulation, but I hated the thought of Nora out in the dark and cold trying to start the damn thing.

Groaning, I swung my legs down from the bed. Rooting around in the dark, I managed to get dressed in my jeans and flannel. I hadn't rearranged my furniture since I moved in years ago, so I didn't need a flashlight until I was ready to go out the back door and fire the generator up. I'd only need to start it, and my place would be heating up in case I had trouble with the house generator and had to relocate Nora.

To my place.

My gut clenched hard, and deceptive excitement wound through me. She'd be in my place for safety reasons and the more that all of me understood the concept, the better.

I got into my winter coat and stuffed a plain black stocking hat on my head. Then I stepped outside. Snow sandblasted me across the face. Wind howled around the buildings. The yard light was off, and everything was dark.

I got the generator going, hit the manual transfer switch, and the light outside the shop came on. Good. The lights made the night feel less ominous. I went through the shed to the front door. I braced myself to step back out again. When I did, I kept going.

The beam from my flashlight didn't cut far into the blustering snow. I had to walk at a tilt to keep the wind from knocking me over, but I reached the house. I plunged through the drifting between the house and garage and finally reached the generator. She had the same model as mine, but despite the oil and fuel levels being okay, the engine refused to turn over.

"Goddammit." I kept going until the cold leached through my gloves to my fingers. My nose was going to freeze and fall off. One last attempt pulling the recoil cord and nothing.

"Dammit, Kira." The woman was stubborn and thought shit should work when she needed it to. Preventive maintenance and care weren't in her vocabulary. She also hadn't known Nora would be staying at the house. It probably wouldn't have mattered.

Was Nora even awake? I'd have to let her know so she didn't risk freezing to come out and try. And so I could get her somewhere warm. The power could be out for hours or days.

A sizable drift had built up in front of the door. I kicked as much as I could out of the way and punched through the rest until I could wedge the door open. The house was quiet. All the appliances were dead in the water, and the furnace was shut down. I couldn't tell how badly the place had cooled off. I could just as well be on the beach after being frozen alive outside.

"Nora?" Her bedroom was upstairs. Maybe she didn't hear me.

I toed my boots off and left my hat and gloves on the bench in the entry. I still dragged enough snow into the house on my jeans and my coat. The stairs creaked as I took them up.

I trained the light on Nora's open door.

"Nora?" I said softly.

I swung the light into the room. Was the bed empty? The old quilt her grandma had made was rumpled, but I couldn't find Nora. Her winter gear was by the door. Was she sleeping on the couch? Finally, I spied a puff of hair sticking out of the top of the blankets. She'd formed her own cove under the covers.

I tapped a lump at the foot of the bed, hoping I hit her leg. "Nora."

She woke with a start, sitting straight up, her hair swirled around her face. "I'm late."

"What?"

She let out a cry, and I held back a laugh. She scrambled toward the head of the bed. She stilled. "Colt? What the hell are you doing in my bedroom?" She shivered. "Holy shit, it's chilly."

I shined the light right on her face to mess with her and tell myself I didn't really want to see how blue her eyes were when she just woke up. "Yeah, sleeping beauty. It's because the power's been out for a while."

She screwed her mouth up and blocked her face from the light. "Okay? I'll try the generator."

"It's dead."

She sighed, the same sound I'd heard over the years directed toward her mother. "Right. Well, I'll close all the bedrooms off and burrow in here. Heat rises, so..."

The decision had to be made. I couldn't rest knowing

she was in the house, shivering in her blankets with nothing to do until the sun was up when she'd shiver with a book. "There is no heat to rise. Get your things. My place should be warming back up."

She didn't move. "Excuse me?"

I quashed the thrill swelling in my chest. I'd diligently kept her—and everyone else—out of my apartment over the years, and it hadn't been easy when she was a nosy kid who was used to everything being hers.

No one had been in my place. Kira didn't even bother to come in. She had given me the keys, said I'd better take care of it all, or I was out, and that was it. I hadn't felt right bringing someone back to my den when very little of the furniture was mine and only because it was included in room and board. If I quit working, I quit having a roof over my head. Being homeless wasn't an option. I was too fucking old to sleep on the streets.

But Nora was coming with me tonight. "Get some things. We're going."

"It's—" She grabbed her phone. "Two in the morning."

"Exactly."

"The power might come back on."

"Then you can return." Otherwise, I wouldn't get a lick of sleep wondering if she was warm enough.

She blew a puff of hair out of her face. She was dressed like she could trek through the woods. Fluffy pajama pants with snowmen on them and a long-sleeved shirt with a giant present on the front. Too late, I realized she didn't have a bra on. The material wasn't enough to hide the sway of her tits.

Lust rammed my gut.

Snowman and Christmas PJs, and I was fighting an erection within seconds.

She curled her cute little feet under her and shivered. "Okay. Fine. Wait—what about the pipes?"

Right. The power outage. "Burst plumbing isn't something we can take care of in the freezing cold with no light. There's enough heat to keep the temp above freezing until morning, and Kira's at least insulated the outdoor faucets."

"Shouldn't I leave the bathtub dripping?"

"Ain't gonna help when it's twenty below. Come on, Nora. The temperature will hold above freezing long enough. We can come back when it's light out." We had all fucking night. All the next day. But I was in a hurry to get her to my place and get her comfortable. Then I could be uncomfortable.

She got out of bed, and I stood by the door, training enough light in the room so she could pack some clothes into a tote bag. On the way downstairs, she ducked into the bathroom and grabbed a few items.

We bundled back up, and I led her outside. The wind almost knocked her over. I caught her and tucked her into my side. Layers of coats and clothing didn't mask how good she felt.

"Oh, wow," she croaked and leaned into me.

I kept her hugged to me as we wove our way to the shop. There was a moment when the snow gusted around us so bad that we had to stop and let it pass until the shop was visible again. If I wasn't so conscientious about the danger, I would've wished to have a little more time with her pressed against me like this.

Finally, I pulled her into the shelter of the shop. She made no move to push away from me. We stood for several moments, catching our breath, her tucked under an arm and me holding the flashlight aimed at the floor.

"You okay?" I asked gruffly.

"Yes. Shitty weather." She sucked in air she didn't have to fight the wind for. The next breath was a yawn.

"Come on." I finally disentangled her from me and strode toward my place at the back without thinking about how empty I now felt without her in my arms. "It's warmer in here."

The shop was heated, but we kept it in the forties. The small generator would have no issues maintaining the shop's temperature. I stored plenty of gas. I hated being in the elements without the basics. When we got to the entry of my living quarters, she paused. Her face glowed in the beam of light bouncing off the door.

"The forbidden realm." She added extra awe in her tone and quirked the corner of her mouth up.

Her humor took the magnitude out of the situation. She needed shelter. I had shelter. That was all. "Haha. Get in, snow angel."

She blinked at the endearment and patted her hat. "I don't want to drag snow in."

I stood dripping on the black mat directly inside my door. "I'll manage around the mess. Get in."

"You're bossy." She stepped in and crowded on the mat with me.

We took our stuff off. I shed my items first so I wouldn't watch her undress like a creep and went to the nightstand by the bed and turned a lamp on.

She clutched her tote bag and looked around. I set the flashlight down and scratched the back of my neck while trying to view my place through her eyes. Technically called a mother-in-law suite, it was more like an economy apartment. My kitchen was a counter along the far wall with an oven, microwave, and fridge. A small table that was a level above the card table was behind the couch with recliner ends that faced the TV. I didn't veg out in front of the screen often. The furniture had been here when I arrived, new and unused, and it was clear which end I preferred thanks to the wear in the cushions and the end table full of my secret addiction—espionage thrillers. Next to them was one of the many pocketknives Nora had given me each year for Christmas since I first arrived.

Overall, not much for a man who'd lived here over sixteen years. Would she find it plain? Sad that I had so little?

Her gaze swept to my bed, and she cocked a brow at me. "Why did I expect a cot?"

I eyed my plush, pillow-top, queen-sized bed that was so tall Nora would probably need a stool or a running start to get into it. The bed was my one main purchase besides my pickup after I'd collected a few paychecks. "My old ass likes comfort."

She laughed, the sound so delighted and light that I could only stare. She was fucking gorgeous. A snow angel was in my place. Among my things. Even worse, in her snowman pajama pants and her Christmas-present shirt with her tote bag hugged in front of her unbound tits, she looked like she belonged.

"Go ahead and take the bed." Damn, I was glad I'd cleaned the place and changed the bedding before I left for my vacation. The old sheets were part of the laundry I was doing when Nora busted me in the buff.

"I'm not kicking you out of your bed. It's not your fault Mom didn't take care of the generator."

"To be fair, she thought she'd be gone." I was used to either ignoring digs at my boss or standing up for her, but sometimes Nora also needed to be reminded her mom was just a person who couldn't think of every possibility, otherwise the hurt would just keep piling up.

She lifted a shoulder. "I'll sleep on the couch."

"My mama would come back from the dead and kick my ass. You're sleeping in the bed. I can change the sheets, but I've only slept in them one and a half nights."

Her eyes were luminous. "Your mom passed away?"

I didn't talk about my mama to anyone. My throat grew unexpectedly tight. "Before I moved to North Dakota."

"I'm sorry."

This time, I lifted a shoulder. I was sorry for a lot. Nora didn't need to be.

"Your dad?" she asked softly.

"I'm in the same boat as you there. The only difference is that my mama didn't run him off. He left on his own."

"That sucks. I'm sorry." This time her apology was more commiseration.

I usually avoided talking about my parents, but I wasn't trying to crawl out of my skin. For once, it was nice to have someone know a little about me. Didn't mean I wanted to rehash my dismal history. "Yeah, well, teen dads don't make the best dads." Not in my world. I swallowed, my past welling up, more wanting to be shared with her. "You can use the bathroom while I grab a couple of extra blankets for the couch."

She gave me a small smile. "Thanks."

When she disappeared into the little bathroom, I dug a pillow and blanket out of the drawer built into the bed frame. I had to get settled before she came out. I could not watch her climb into my bed or nestle in my sheets with that spun-gold hair on my pillow. I could not see how right she looked there when I knew it was wrong in so many ways.

* * *

Nora

. . .

I pulled the blankets to my chin. They smelled like him. Dial soap and fabric softener. Soft smells.

I'd been out with a few guys I couldn't bring myself to go on date number two with. They might've been nice. We might've had a connection. But their cologne stunk. Too strong. Too artificial. And while the perfumes in soap and fabric softener weren't any better, they intertwined in my brain with a gruff man who braved a blizzard to drag me back to his place so I could be warmer.

Getting pulled out of a deep sleep wasn't terrible when Colt was the one holding the flashlight.

I stifled a yawn. I'd heard no movement from the couch since I'd killed the light from the lamp. Adrenaline coursed through my veins thanks to waking up thinking I was late for a final in college, then finding Colt in my room and getting bitch-slapped by Mother Nature for a hundred yards.

Trying not to be noisy, I rolled over. Then rolled the other way.

"Can't sleep?" His deep rumble from only ten feet away was a massage for my ears. I could listen to him talk all night and every night. Colt was a guy who sat back and let everyone else do the speaking unless he had something to say. I'd heard him talk more the last few days than I can remember. Usually, he said his piece and then got the hell away from me.

"No, I'm too wired."

"Worried?"

"Not really." I should be. What if the pipes burst and the house flooded? Mom would blame me. She'd tell everyone it was my fault.

What if the power didn't come back on tomorrow? Or the next day? How much fuel did Colt have?

Would I have to stay with him for days? Sleep more than once in sheets that smelled like him?

He fell quiet, and I took the invite to keep talking. And to get nosy. He'd opened up about his parents, and I craved more. "Where did you go last week?"

I heard a slow inhale. Would he answer?

I was about to roll over again to attempt sleep when he said, "Idaho."

My thoughts about where he disappeared to varied, but I'd settled on him holing up in a hotel in a town not far away where he'd have a little more privacy than he did in Coal Haven. Hearing he traveled so far was...odd. Unexpected. What was in Idaho? "Really?"

"Yes."

Again, he went silent.

Okay. I'd gotten more tidbits on him than ever before. I was being greedy.

"It's where I'm from," he said quietly. I'd thought a lot about where he was from. Mom said she met him at a gas station in Montana. That was it. I had no more information from him, so I assumed he was from Montana.

I bit my lower lip. He couldn't see my grin, but I didn't want him to sense my triumph. He really was the perfect employee for Mom. Quiet. Proficient. Minded his own damn business, unlike I was doing. "I thought Mom conjured you from thin air."

"I prefer it that way."

I frowned, rolling to my back and lacing my fingers over my stomach. "I wish you didn't. You know all my dark secrets."

"Like how the idiot you were dating over the summer was taking money from your baristas' tip jar?"

I let out an indignant gasp. "How do you know about

that?" My cheeks grew hot. Holden might've told him. How embarrassing. "He was...a letdown."

"They all are. You have terrible taste in men, Nora."

I flopped to my side and propped myself on an elbow. Residual light from the time glowing on the microwave made the couch a dark blob in the middle of the room. "I do not." I thought about the guys I'd dated. "Ugh. Okay, I *might.*"

His dry chuckle filled the room. "Wiener Dog Guy?"

Had Holden bitched to Colt about all my crap experiences? The two were close, and I hated to think Colt knew just how dismal my dating life was. But at the same time...he'd listened and obviously remembered. And he was on my side. I clung to the warmth the thought caused and recalled Wiener Dog Guy. Nick liked to talk about his wiener dog. He never called the dog by name. *My wiener dog this. My wiener dog that.*

Then I found out he didn't have a wiener dog. He didn't have a dog at all. He liked saying wiener. A lot. "One instance. Two with Tip Jar Guy."

"Kiss Your Best Friend Guy?"

Creepy dates weren't as bad as the dates who'd passed me over for someone else. Hannah had been one of my only friends in high school, and she'd helped me find a prom date. That date had kissed her when I was driving her date home after the dance because I was the only one with a vehicle. Hannah pushed him away and told me the next day.

"My first clue should've been how he let another girl wear his tux coat for the whole dance."

"He did not," Colt growled.

My shiver wasn't from the chill or even the delightful rumble. He was incensed for me. I had been left feeling like not good enough once again and had only told Holden. I'd made him swear not to do anything to my prom date.

It was likely a coincidence the date's tires had all deflated while he was out of town for a track meet.

"Yep, he did. It didn't dawn on me later that he wasn't being chivalrous and that the tux girl was trying to steal him." I'd been happy to go to prom and told myself I didn't care. Too bad those memories overshadowed the experience.

"Because it shouldn't have been something you had to worry about." Anger still radiated from his voice. "If it was my daughter, I would've hunted that bastard down and gutted him for hurting her."

"I bet you'd be a good dad."

The silence fell hard and heavy. Was he touchy about his age or his single status? Did he want kids but couldn't stand someone long enough to have them with her? "Colt?"

"I guess we'll never know."

Okay, then. I detected a sense of loss that echoed inside of me as if he could understand the idea of a family that never happened. "I wanted kids. A lot of them." He knew a lot about me, but I never told anyone my feelings on family. I'd wanted to create one with a man, and none of the men I'd dated had come close to my not-so-low-key obsession with Colt. "I wanted to be the kind of mom I never had."

"You will be."

I snorted. "Not if I keep finding Tip Jar Guys."

"Just make sure the next All Organic Guy doesn't hoard Pop-Tarts."

Burrowing into his scent, I smiled. "He didn't hoard them." I'd only found ten boxes stashed in his bathroom closet. Along with a few packages of Hostess snack cakes.

I thought the poor guy had an eating disorder, but no. He was a pathological liar, and the food wasn't only one instance where he lied. He made Weiner Dog Guy look truthful.

The easy silence between me and Colt should be left

alone, but I liked talking with him. My eyelids were droopy, but I continued to pry. "Why don't you talk about your life before Coal Haven?"

His breathing was quiet. Had he fallen asleep?

A few moments went by. "I'm not proud of it, snow angel."

I smiled at the nickname. "Were you in jail?" I joked. Honestly, jail time would be less troubling than some of my exes' antics.

"I've been in jail, yes, but that's only part of it."

Oh. Shocked, I nibbled my lip. I hadn't expected him to admit so much. But he did, and he said jail, not prison. Curiosity pumped more adrenaline into my veins. "What for?"

"Stupid shit, Nora. I was a stupid kid doing stupid things, and I didn't know how to stop."

"Meeting Mom made you stop?" I thought of Mom differently. She wouldn't lift a finger to help her family, but if she aided strangers, then maybe she had a soft spot somewhere in her withered heart.

"No. She helped me decide to quit giving up." The blankets on the couch rustled. "Good night, Nora."

And that was it. The door was slammed shut in my face, leaving me in the cold even as I was tucked into his warm bed. Disappointed and a little hurt, I wasn't able to fall right to sleep. I had a lot to think about. The mystery of Colt had only grown bigger. I wished he'd let me all the way in, but not even I could think of a reason why he should.

Three

COLT

I woke before Nora and left her huddled under my blankets while I ignored the satisfaction inside me at seeing her in my bed. She was usually an early riser, but being up in the middle of the night for a couple of hours left her sleeping in again.

Why couldn't I keep my mouth shut?

I'd almost told her too much. She'd never look at me the same. A part of me had grown fond of the hero worship I caught in her gaze. I wasn't a piece of shit to someone like her.

Her mom didn't look at me like she remembered the dirty, grimy Colt she'd plucked out of the gutter, but I knew that she knew. Nora didn't. Holden didn't. None of the Barrons and no one in this town. Between the anonymity and the money I earned, this job was everything I needed and more than I could've asked for.

Chores were done. Nora had popped out before I'd gotten to the horses. The wind was still blowing, and snow continued to fall. We couldn't talk, but we both knew what had to be done. We made tracks where we needed to, dug out what had been buried, and got all the animals fed and watered. Digging out the driveway and around the doors would take a full day, maybe two, once the wind died down, which wasn't supposed to happen for another two or three days.

I heated up a frozen pizza while Nora showered. To keep myself from thinking about her naked in my bathroom with her long, golden-brown hair hanging down her back, I went outside, checked my generator, and tried to beat Kira's into submission.

No luck. I might have another night with Nora under my roof while I confessed to what an utter piece of shit I was. Emotions warred inside me, the battle for liking that she'd be under my roof for longer against the fear I couldn't keep my mouth shut.

I went inside, took off my snow gear, and inhaled the scent of fake cheese and bland crust. "Goddammit."

Nora came out of the bathroom. She wore a fuzzy red sweater that said "Deck the halls all night long" and black leggings that would only fuel dirty fantasies with the way they molded around her calves and thighs. Her hair was wound into one of my towels, and a low burn ignited in my gut. A stark desire awakened to remind me of what I'd fucked up and what I should never have. A woman. A home. A life that wasn't about making money and sending it away.

"What's wrong?" she asked, those blue eyes pinning me in place.

"I don't have any non-dairy, gluten-free, granola shit." I

nearly winced. I didn't mean to make it sound like I didn't care about her dietary needs or showcase how uncultured I was. Normally, being a working Joe didn't bother me, but she was a business owner. A chef. A baker. An entrepreneur.

"I'll be fine," she reassured me. "A slice won't kill me."

"But you—"

"Colt. It's fine. I've healed a lot and can tolerate some dairy and gluten shit." She smiled like she was letting me know she wasn't offended.

But her attempt wasn't good enough. "No, it's not. It'll make you sick. I'll run to the house. We should rescue all the produce you bought anyway."

"I can go." She started for the door.

"Your hair is wet."

She gave me a droll look. "They make these things called hats."

"Ha ha, smart-ass. Stay here." The oven dinged. Good. She might actually listen to me if she had something to do. "Can you get that out? I'll be right back."

She narrowed her eyes at me as she yanked her coat off the hook by the door. "You know I hate being treated like I can't do anything."

I lifted the coat from her hand. "There's a difference between people treating you like you can't do anything and people who want to take care of you."

Her lips parted. Yeah, I'd heard what I said, but I refused to take it back. I wanted to take care of her. She wasn't mine, but I'd still watch out for her.

The trip to the house didn't take long. I grabbed some plastic bags from Kira's stash and loaded up as many of Nora's groceries as I could carry. I took the first batch over.

With my face half frozen, I went back for the rest. It was clear what was Nora's and what was Kira's. Kira hated cooking, and she practically drank straight creamer with a dash of Folgers. The cupboards were either empty or filled with flour and sugar that could be donated to the Coal Haven Historical Society.

I hauled everything into the apartment. Nora was at the fridge, her ass hanging out. Of course, I remembered how she'd found me, stark fucking naked with my dick swinging. What would it have been like to find her bare-assed? And when she would turn—

I dropped half of her bags. "I got everything." I put the rest down to turn and took my coat, gloves, and hat off. By the time I got my blood rerouted, Nora had piled her groceries on the table.

"Thank you. You didn't have to do this. Most of the stuff would've been okay." She held up a bag of powder that had a picture of almonds on the front. "I was going to make macarons to bring to Holden's for Christmas. Maybe I'll still have time."

"Has he checked in with you?"

Her smile was fond. "Of course. They're doing good. The whole town is out of power. He gets the alerts from the power company, and it's still too bad to send their crews out."

I nodded. I expected as much. "As long as we know that. The house is cold, but with the entry closed and the plastic Kira put on the picture windows, the temperature is holding in the high forties. Downstairs at least."

Relief crossed her face. "Oh, good." She took out the food that needed to be refrigerated. "Do you want any of this with your pizza?"

The hesitancy in her question gutted me. She'd been given so much shit for cooking, baking, and eating differently. Yeah, sometimes her healthed-up brownies tasted like chalk smeared on cardboard, but she wasn't forcing the food on anyone or doling out lectures about how uncivilized we were.

I tipped my head toward the little round containers she held. "What's that?"

"Coconut yogurt." She bit her lower lip. "Remember when I tried making my own?"

"I thought that was cottage cheese."

Her grimace was amused. "I don't know what it turned into. I buy my yogurt these days—dairy-free."

"Don't want to have explosive diarrhea in my bathroom?"

Her face flushed. "Do you have to know everything?"

I stifled a grin. "Two plus two, Nora. What else would dairy do to you?"

"Do you really want to know about the mucus production?"

This time I laughed. "Got it. I'll pass."

She smiled, but she'd tipped her head to the side and was studying me, her expression full of wonder.

I sobered. I wasn't the type of guy to give her that look. "What?"

"I don't think I've seen you really laugh."

"I don't deserve to laugh."

She recoiled, and I suppressed a groan. The response had been instinctive. Shit had been slipping from my mouth left and right the last two days.

"Why would you say that?" She set the yogurt down and crossed to me, then planted her hands on her hips.

"Nora—"

She held up a hand. "You're going to make excuses. I'm going to disagree. So let me just say this. You are a good man, Colt. I don't know what you were like before, but since I've known you, you've been a good guy. Even all your hookups gush about how cool you are."

I'd never been so thankful for my beard. My face heated, and the facial hair covered half my blush. Hearing Nora talk about the women I'd been with was embarrassing and only added to my shame. No, I didn't lead women on. I didn't ghost them either. I did the bare minimum, and yet I was touted as the hero one-night-stander of Coal Haven.

"You're honorable," she continued.

Son of a bitch. Was I full-on blushing?

"You're thoughtful, and you work really damn hard. You don't only care for me and my family but all the animals and then some." She stepped closer. "I think you even give all those barn cats a lot of belly scritches."

The flush would ignite my skin if she continued complimenting me. "Nora, you don't know me."

She laid a hand flat on my chest. My breathing turned shallow.

"*You* don't know you." She was adamant. "Did you know guilt is meant to teach you a lesson, and once you've learned from it, you need to crumple it up and throw it away because it's done its job?" She was inches from me, as close as we'd been when I carried her to the house.

"Who told you that?"

"I went to a lot of counseling when I was in college. I almost went into it for a career, but I didn't want to be in an office all day."

I stroked my gaze over her, content to be this close and have a reason to study her pert little nose, the handful of freckles barely visible on her creamy skin, and the perfect bow her mouth made. I brushed my thumb over an old acne scar. I remember wishing she could get some help. Her skin had looked so inflamed and painful, but Kira just claimed Nora didn't wash her face enough. I was acutely aware I knew fuck all about teenage girls and had kept out from between them as much as I could.

"I'm glad you found help," I said.

"I wish you would've, too, so you'd think better about yourself."

"Angel, you're too good for a man like me." I yanked my hand back like I'd touched a hot burner. I needed to keep my damn mouth shut.

"But I'm not," she insisted. "And you're not too old."

"Yes. I am." I'd never been more sure of anything.

"Prove it." Those pouty lips of hers stuck out in clear challenge.

I'd opened up too much, and it was too late to slam the lid back down. The only thing I could do was open it far enough for her to see the garbage. As much as I didn't want to drive her away now that she was getting closer, I had to. She had to know why my attraction to her wasn't right.

"Because you're almost the same age as my daughter."

* * *

Nora

Oh.

My.

God.

Daughter. Colt had a daughter.

If it was my daughter, I would've hunted that bastard down and gutted him for hurting her.

He'd been serious. He hadn't been speaking hypothetically.

A daughter.

He deliberately stepped away, his gaze dropping to the floor, and he went to a drawer by the sink and withdrew the pizza cutter.

The cardboard pizza was probably cold.

I spun on a heel to keep him in my sights. "You're going to drop that bomb and go about your business?"

"Plan to."

I let out a sardonic laugh. "No. I mean, it's none of my business, but seriously. You have a kid?"

"I wasn't part of her life."

Wasn't. He was speaking plainly, but the door to his emotions was sealed shut. I saw nothing in his gaze.

"Are you now?" I asked.

He lifted a shoulder, his broad back to me. "I don't fit in anywhere with her now."

Pieces were clicking into place. "Is that why you came home early? You felt out of place?"

He shoved a hand through his hair. His flush from earlier had faded, and loss and regret lingered in his eyes. "The food's getting cold."

"We can eat and talk." I folded my arms. He brushed his fingers against his thumbs, his arms hanging at his sides. Over and over. He was nervous. I should drop it, but holding everything in couldn't be good. "Why keep her to yourself?"

He drew his brows together. "Do the math, Nora."

I didn't have his daughter's age, but if we were close, his point wasn't hard to figure out. "You were a teen when she was born."

"I was a piece of shit. In and out of juvie. I broke up with her mother as soon as she told me she was pregnant. Said it wasn't my problem." He stuffed another hand into his hair and paced. "The only good thing I did was diligently use protection after so I didn't become a deadbeat dad to another unfortunate kid."

He was selling himself short. Whatever he'd been like before, he wasn't that man now. "She's doing well though?"

He stopped, a beam of pride shone from his face a moment before it was buried. "Yeah. She, uh, had a baby."

I tossed my hands into the air, excitement coursing through me. "Oh. My. God. You're a *grandpa*? That's amazing!"

His expression turned stricken. "I'm not a grandpa any more than I'm a dad."

"You are too." I poked him in the shoulder, still grinning. A grandpa! "You wouldn't have gone there for the holidays if you weren't part of their lives."

"I'm not." He paced again, propping his hands loosely on his hips. Colt brimmed with emotion. He probably wasn't used to feelings. "I'm just the guy who's been sending money for the last fifteen-some years."

"Sixteen and a half. I was thirteen when you arrived." I snapped my fingers. "Is that why you were weird around me?"

He gave me a funny look. "You were a kid, and I was a grown man. Yeah, I went out of my way to not be creepy or have people wonder if you were safe around me. If you're asking if you reminded me of my daughter, then no, you were just *a* kid, and I was only thinking of *my* kid."

I'd overheard my uncles asking Mom what she was thinking, bringing some ranch hand home when she had a young daughter. She said if Colt couldn't be trusted, she'd deal with him herself and they'd never find the body. Sometimes, she could surprise me that she actually cared.

I smiled. "Thank you for not being creepy." And I was glad he didn't equate me with his kid. Our age difference was hard enough for him to get over.

He stopped, his intense gaze striking me. "I've been pretty fucking creepy the last two days."

Awareness traced down my spine, and hope retraced the path back up. "What are you saying?"

"Fuck. Nothing." He yanked a chair out. "Let's eat."

"Colt—"

"Let's fucking eat, Nora."

I drew back. He'd hit his limit of sharing, and when it came to me, he'd rather close me out. I'd respect it. "What else do you want with your yogurt and cold pizza?"

Four

COLT

I'd spent all afternoon moving snow that was blowing right back in.

Why the hell did I open my big mouth? I'd gone sixteen and a half years without telling a soul about my daughter. Then I'd spilled it to the woman I was lusting after who was almost the same age.

Nora was a couple years older, thank fuck, or I'd be castrating myself with the clamp pliers. Other guys might be okay getting horny over women their kid's age, but I wasn't one of them.

I thought of the erection I'd suffered the first night Nora was here.

Guess I was one of those guys.

I pulled the walk-behind snowblower I used to clean up around the doorways into the shop and turned to close the door. A nice drift had already blown in on the floor inside the door, but it'd wait until the wind died down. In a day or two.

A light in the house was on.

I almost hit the button to close the smaller door in the shop, but I paused. The power was back on. I jogged across the driveway, my face tucked into the collar of my coat.

I took a few minutes to run through the place and make sure nothing had frozen and leaked and that the furnace would kick back on. It did. Nora would be able to return to the house.

And I'd have the loneliest night of my damn life.

One time with her in my bed—and I wasn't even in it—and I'd quickly gotten addicted to having her around. To talking in the middle of the night. Sharing secrets I had no business spilling.

I went back to my place. Entering, I was enveloped by savory smells. Nora was at the stove, reading one of my books and slowly stirring something in a pot, her stockinged foot acting like a kickstand against her other leg.

She glanced over her shoulder and smiled.

Everything I didn't deserve stood in my kitchen, looking all sexy yet adorable and domestic.

My chest grew tight, and drawing breath became hard. I forced out a "Power's on."

"Oh." She switched her attention to the pot. "I was just making some soup for tonight. Mind if I hang out until it's done? Then I suppose you want your place back to yourself."

I wanted her in my space. I wanted her asking personal questions I was compelled to answer. I wanted her to keep not being scared off when I told her what a shit show I'd been in my younger years.

But she wasn't mine to have. I still needed this job. I hadn't done right by my daughter, and I'd argue I never did, but now I had a granddaughter. I couldn't disgust them by lusting after my boss's daughter and disgust them by ending my career.

The oven dinged. She set the book on the counter and abandoned the soup. When she bent to get a pan out of the oven, I didn't drag my gaze away. I'd warned her I was being a creep.

Her thighs flexed, and her ass rounded and damn. My fingers curled. I could dig into those lush hips and thrust—

I spun away. "After we eat, the house should be warmed up." I fled to the bathroom to wash up before she withdrew the pan of something that smelled good and found me leering at her ass.

I splashed water on my face and eyed myself in the mirror. My cheeks were still red from the outside, my hair messed up from the hat, and my beard needed a trim. More than that, I saw the lines winging out from my eyes. I was almost one and a half decades older than the woman in my kitchen.

It didn't matter if Nora was thirty. Kira would have opinions. No one was good enough for Nora. According to Kira, no one could protect Nora from herself. When she'd hired me, she'd said, "I catch you trying to dig into my family and make yourself one of us, you're gone. You understand? I need ranch help, not another fucking family member. You treat the cows good and keep to yourself, or that's it."

Kira had given me a lane to stay in and a reason not to get out. But Nora made me want to take the exit on two wheels.

"Get a hold of yourself," I growled. I had no money and a granddaughter who didn't need a worthless grandpa.

Grandpa. Fuck me.

In the kitchen, I sat in my normal chair. Nora had

already set the table and dished out what looked like chicken tortilla soup. A bowl full of crunchy chips sat in the middle of the table. I'd eaten with the family before, but this was the first time a meal had been prepared just for me. My chest grew tight.

She pushed the chips toward me. "Homemade corn tortilla chips." Her lips curved. "Gluten-free."

"Thanks."

"I wasn't sure if you liked chicken. There's a lot of beef in your freezer."

"One of my benefits." My only benefit. Kira was a fair employer, but she wasn't generous.

I was several bites in before I noticed Nora stirred her soup in one direction, then the other, not taking a bite.

I set my spoon down and rubbed my hands on my legs. Did she notice my reaction? Had she caught on I was desperate for her to stay, but I needed her to leave more? "Something on your mind?"

Her gaze softened. "I've pried enough already."

The food churned in my gut. More of my past. I couldn't deny her much. Just myself. "Go ahead."

She took a fortifying breath. "What's your daughter's name?"

The question had likely been gnawing at her since I'd snapped at her before lunch. I never talked about my daughter. To anyone. The girl hadn't gotten any of my garbage, and that was more than I could've hoped for. "Brittany."

"And your granddaughter?"

My heart nearly burst out of my damn chest. My granddaughter was a baby. She didn't know me as a deadbeat dad, and I'd work hard to make her proud to be related to me. To not regret her connection to me at the very least. "Berkley. Her dad's a B-name too. Ben."

"Brittany, Ben, and Berkley. I bet they're a cute family."

"Yeah." I stuffed a chip into my mouth. The groan slipped out. Still warm with a hint of salt. I chowed chips and salsa as much as the next guy, but this one chip ruined all the shit in town for me. When I caught Nora's gaze, she was smirking.

"My cooking skills have gotten better, yeah?"

"I'll say." I snagged another chip. I devoured two bowls of soup and half the bowl of chips before I slowed down.

When she finished her food, she pushed her bowl to the side and stretched her hands high above her head. "I guess I'll pack up and get going."

I didn't want her to leave. A big fucking sign that said she should. "I can help."

"You've been working all afternoon, and I've almost finished an entire book." There was a wistful note to her smile. "I don't remember when I last read a book in a day. The shop keeps me so busy."

"You like it."

"I love it." She traced her finger on the top of the table. "More than I thought I would. I meet so many people and..." She chewed on her lower lip, and I couldn't take my gaze off her mouth, hoping for a flash of pink tongue. "People treat me differently than they do here. When I helped Uncle Cameron with the farmers' market, I was under his command. Everyone deferred to him, and he got the accolades if something we tried was a hit. But with Bean Good, it's all me. Sure, there are complaints but so many compliments. Not just on my food, but how I do business."

"It's about time." Another reason I couldn't act on my body's reaction to her. She was better off away from Coal Haven.

"Mom would say it's gone to my head." Rising, she gathered our bowls.

I refused to let her wait on me. I'd been raised better. No

matter how I'd acted, I had learned how to behave properly. Hopefully, my mother could look down and be proud.

"Holden asked me about opening a second shop," she said at the sink.

"Are you?"

"No." She let out a soft chuckle. "Another shop in the same town would be stressful. I'd have to do a ton of market research. And a second place in another town would stretch me too thin."

Nora was a go-getter. If she didn't think a second coffee shop was a good idea, she was likely making a well-informed decision. Yet I detected a quick brush-off like she was afraid to grow too fast too soon. I didn't push her. She was the one with schooling and experience. She must have a reason for being cautious.

When the dishes were washed, she started putting all her winter gear on. I did the same and ignored her protests. She wasn't carrying all the bags over on her own. She'd only packed a few things for breakfast, claiming the power might go out again since the wind was still brutal. I didn't want the power to go out again, but seeing her leave wasn't the relief I hoped it would be.

I walked her to the house, training the flashlight through the throng of flakes that made it hard to see where we were going. "This makes me think we should tie ropes to ourselves or something like in the old days!" Nora shouted over the wind.

I wrenched open the door for her and held on tight to keep it from slamming against the house and coming off its hinges. Maybe she should've stayed another night.

My shoulder was already aching at the thought of another day on the couch, but the rest of me wanted her to stay in my bed.

She turned, waiting for me to enter, but I didn't. Hope

faded in those cornflower irises. "Text me when you get back."

I nodded and wrestled the door shut. Walking back, her words played through my head. When was the last time anyone had been concerned about my safety?

* * *

Nora

The power was out again. I checked the time on my phone. Four in the morning. I snuggled further into the blankets. The house was cozy. I'd pumped the heat higher than normal in case the power was lost again. The extra heat would stick around for a while.

But I also didn't want Colt venturing out in the storm with no yard lights to get me.

Should I go over there?

The wind howled outside, stronger than before, making the boards creak like the whole place was swaying back and forth. The house had withstood a lot of storms, but I'd always hated the sound.

If I tried to go to the shop, I'd probably get lost and find myself on the other side of the highway and freeze to death. Mom would tell the town I should've known better.

Or she might blame Colt and fire him. I'd gladly take the blame.

I shot off a message to him. **Power's out, but it's still warm. I'll wait until daylight before I come over if the power stays out.**

There. I put the phone back on the nightstand and closed my eyes.

My phone buzzed. And buzzed again.

I grabbed it and squinted. Colt.

Had he ever called me? I answered with a chipper, "Good morning."

"Fuck, did I wake you?"

"Colt, I just texted you."

His grumpy grunt was back in full effect. "You sure you're doing okay?"

"I'm fine. I don't want either of us to risk the trip. Sorry I woke you though."

Another grunt. "I was awake."

"Why?"

"Couldn't sleep."

I giggled. "That's usually how it works."

A soft huff came over the line. "I was thinking."

"Did you get any rest?"

"Enough."

So that meant he got not one wink. "I'll do chores in the morning. You sleep."

"You're not doing chores alone in the blizzard."

"You do."

"No one needs to worry about me, snow angel."

"No one might need to, but I do." I was met with silence. "Don't you believe me?"

What sounded like a resigned sigh came over the line. "I don't know what to believe when it comes to you, Nora."

I wasn't sure what we were talking about. We'd danced around the topic. Was he attracted to me? After his outburst about being creepy and then when he'd eyed my mouth like he wanted to devour me, I started to wonder...could he be into me? Like, really into me? Was he fighting himself and how wrong he thought this was?

Was he afraid of my mother? I'd always seen his compliance as a way of not caring, of not wishing to get involved in family drama. Was he afraid of creating his own drama?

Did I want to pursue a guy who was so conflicted about me?

I didn't have an answer, but I didn't want to quit hearing his voice in my ear in the hours before dawn. "Colt, if your daughter's grown, why are you still working the ranch?"

"I don't have any other job skills."

"There are a lot of ranches."

"I don't need a gap of employment on my record."

I hadn't thought of that as a concern, but I'd known I was getting a hefty amount of money. I'd had the privilege of not needing to find a job. "Has Mom given you a raise even once?" His silence was enough of an answer. *Dammit, Mom.* He was a good worker, but she'd justify his salary as not needing a cost of living when he got room and board. "You should ask for one."

His low chuckle came through the line. "You think that'll go over well?" He was right there. "I got what I need. My pickup's paid off. I get beef and gas from the ranch. The rest goes to Brittany."

"Still?"

"I had a lot of years to make up for. Brittany was almost a teen before she and her mama got a dime from me. Now, it all goes to Berkley. It's the least I can do."

I could hear the pride in his voice, but he was continuing to compensate for being gone much of his daughter's life. He was giving them all his dimes, and he would continue to do so until the day he died. But he'd left early when he visited them? I didn't know his family. Maybe they'd rather have the money, but I doubted it. Colt was a guy you wanted around, and I wasn't saying that because I'd made him the focus of all my fantasies. "How's your ex? Do you two get along?"

"Good, and she was more forgiving than she had a right

to be. She remarried when Brittany was eight. The guy's real good to her. He's a proper father."

I winced. He was hard on himself and I understood, but it was hard to hear. "And that's why you came home early? You saw your grandkid, and the rest was too much?"

"They're never too much."

Meaning he wasn't enough. He felt out of place. Useless, like he'd said earlier. I wouldn't talk him out of his feelings, but I could lighten the conversation. "I hate that you weren't comfortable enough to hang out longer, but I'm glad I caught your little fridge show."

"Jesus, Nora. Don't remind me."

I laughed. "Oh, I'll be reminding myself. That was an impressive view."

"Woman, you're gonna kill me. Your mom would kill me. Holden too."

I'd never tell. A naked Colt was my secret. "Holden would laugh his ass off and then he'd tell Stetson so they could both chortle like schoolboys together."

"I'd never live it down."

Still grinning, I said, "Your full frontal is just between us. Your secrets are safe with me, Colt. All of them."

"Appreciate it," he said all low and growly. I had to close my eyes and let the tingles sweep through me. "Good night. Get some rest."

"Keep your ass in bed and let me do chores." He disconnected.

He was going to be out before I was.

I let out a gusty sigh. My body thrummed, and I pictured a shirtless Colt in bed with that beard that filled me with so many questions.

I'd never dated a guy with a beard. A few of them couldn't grow much facial hair, but I'd seen Colt shaved once. I'd nearly died and came back to life again. It should be against the law to hide that strong jaw, but then the next day, the dark stubble was back, giving me all new thoughts and considerations entirely.

What did a beard feel like between my legs? Would he run it up my thigh and catapult me to the ceiling before my clit was even teased?

I went to sleep with the view of his marble ass in the opening of the fridge, hoping the power would stay out for another day so I could hang out with him.

Five

COLT

I didn't let her do chores alone, but I hadn't beaten her to them. She'd made sure to rise early and be out early. With the power still out, I started the generator, gave up on the dead one by the house, and Nora was parked back in my apartment.

My feet were kicked up in the recliner, and I was reading. Nora was curled on the other side of the couch, wearing leggings and another gaudy Christmas sweater. She'd thrown flourless brownies in the oven, and the smell taunted my nose and my stomach. I'd tasted her first attempts at baking brownies that wouldn't make her sick. These already smelled better.

When the oven was done, she unfurled her legs from the couch. I stared out of the corner of my eye. Long legs. Graceful. Confident. She was all woman, and it was getting impossible not to notice every second I was around her.

Even worse, I liked her. Her witty humor. The way she

defended me. Ask her mom for a raise? Was she crazy? Kira would laugh, thinking I cracked my first joke. I appreciated the sentiment, but I wasn't risking what I had. I had enough money to send to my family. I'd lived on less. Much less.

Nora set the hot pan on the counter. Had my oven ever baked a dessert? "Ice cream would go really well with this." She folded her arms and propped her foot against her other leg again. "You ever made snow cream?"

"'Scuse me?"

"Fresh snow with sugar and cream? It's like ice cream—with a snow aftertaste."

"I wouldn't trust snow flying around a ranch."

Her laughter was everything I never thought I'd hear in my home. "True. But I can have a little cream and sugar without bothering my stomach. I should buy some when I can get to town next."

And suddenly I was like a kid who got to do the special science experiment. I could be the one to get the supplies, surprise her with them, load a bowl with the whitest, freshest snow I could find, and watch her face while she tried it. I'd watch a scoop disappear between those pink lips, and I'd wish I was the fucking spoon.

We had just sat down to a partially cooled brownie, the first decadent bite melting on my tongue the way I wanted Nora to when my phone rang.

I stilled and caught Nora's questioning gaze. The person who called me the most was Kira. I took my phone out of my shirt pocket.

"Mom?" Nora asked. She casually took a bite of a surprisingly good brownie like it wasn't a big deal she was in my home baking and cooking and talking to me in the middle of the night.

"Yeah." I cleared my throat and answered, "Colt here."

"You hear about the fucking storm?" Kira's voice was a whip snap.

"Yes, ma'am. I'm actually—"

"I called Holden, and he said Nora's home. Tell me you went back early like you said you might."

"I'm here. I came back early."

"What the fuck was she thinking? Now you've got her to take care of. And Holden said the power was out?"

I looked to Nora. She was eating her dessert. How much could she hear? I couldn't tell by her neutral expression.

Holden wouldn't lie to his mom. He and Nora would lie by omission, but they knew when to be truthful to keep their mom's trust. Or where Nora was concerned, to keep her mom from questioning every facet of her life.

I pushed back from the table and wandered into the shop so Nora wouldn't hear her mother cuss up a storm. The cold of the concrete floor bled through my socks. "The power came back on last night and then went out again. The house got heated up before it went out again though."

"Meanwhile, Nora's freezing her ass off."

Fuck. "No, ma'am. She's here." I wouldn't lie to her either.

"Where's here?" Kira snapped.

"My place. I got my generator running. Yours wouldn't start."

Icy silence filled the line. I pinched the bridge of my nose. I'd done nothing wrong, but I'd seen what happened when people got on Kira's bad side.

"Just what's going on?"

I struggled not to sound like a delinquent teen trying to justify to the cops the illegal shit I did that I knew was wrong. "We're weathering the storm."

"At your place. She sleeping in your bed or on the floor, Colt?"

"I'm on the couch, Kira." My irritation was rising. I envisioned stomping it down. Kira deserved answers. This was her place, and I was her employee. But didn't over sixteen years of a pristine record and nothing but hard work count for anything?

"Don't goddamn touch her."

"I don't plan to." My gut ached like she'd physically hit me. I'd worked hard to be a guy mothers wouldn't warn their daughters about.

"She might have different plans, and that spoiled little girl gets what she wants."

I snorted out a laugh before common sense told me to hold it in. "She's no spoiled little girl, Kira. You raised her."

"What the hell is that supposed to mean?"

When it came to Nora, I was apparently willing to torch my self-preservation. I had to save face. "It means she's worked hard for everything she has. You taught her well."

"I didn't give her the millions that were handed to her in the trust. Are you and her—"

"No," I said quickly. I had to rescue this conversation. If Kira lashed out, I could end up jobless and homeless at Christmas. Not a good look to my family. "No, ma'am. Your daughter has more sense than to go for a guy like me. I ain't got nothing to give her." The truth hit me in the middle of the chest and sat there, branding into my skin.

"That girl has had a thing for you forever. Why do you think she dates pussies?"

I almost puffed my damn chest out. The losers Nora found were because of me? A form of self-sabotage so she wouldn't find someone else to settle down with? I shouldn't get an ego stroke from the thought. "Nothing's going on."

"And it'd better stay that way, Colt. You're my employee. I don't need more family."

My family was growing, and it was the best damn thing

to see. I might be an outsider looking in, but I'd never want my daughter to have fewer people who loved her around her. I didn't get Kira's reasoning, but I'd abided by her rules since I'd met her. I was the hired guy, and I was lucky to be that. "Got it."

"You'd better. Or I'll take you back to the gas station where I found you." She hung up.

I ground my teeth together. Sixteen years and she would toss me away. After all I'd done for her.

It was getting harder to remind myself I didn't deserve more. Especially with a compassionate woman who raced me to chores and slept in the cold so I wouldn't have to go out in the dark in a blizzard again.

I took a few moments to cool down, letting the cold leach further into my body. In the summer, I kept my boots on, but the socks and the brownies were the coziest I'd been with a woman in my entire life. I was quickly becoming accustomed.

I made enough to send money to my family. I'd die working the ranch, but I'd leave the world giving my kid and her family a better life and a dad and grandpa they didn't regret remembering.

I went inside in time to see Nora with a phone to her ear and hear her say, "Homeless?"

I froze. My world slowed, giving the blizzard outside time to freeze me in place. When Nora's wide gaze rose to mine, my entire being shattered. Kira called her daughter to spill the rest of my dirty secrets.

"Homeless at a gas station?" Nora asked.

Fuck me. I kicked the door closed behind me.

"Okay, but he's not homeless anymore." Nora's back was stiff, her stubborn expression in place. "And last I checked, this ranch isn't a gas station."

Goddamn. She was standing up for me. My chest

pinched until my heart barely had room to beat. I could imagine what Kira was saying. I got room and board. I didn't have a place for myself. I didn't have savings or a retirement plan. I was a poor choice for any woman, and that was why I left my relationships at quick fucks when I got tired of thrusting into my hand.

"I'm still an adult, Mom. So is he. I'm not sure why—"

I couldn't make out Kira's tirade, but her voice rang through the phone.

Nora held the phone out. Then she put it back to her ear. "All right. When the storm lets up, I'll leave. And I won't come back, Mom. I'm tired of your abuse. And I really think you're at least sixteen cost-of-living raises behind with Colt. You should treat your employees better. Uncle Cameron might be an asshole, but his employees love him. Have a great trip. I love you, but don't call me again."

A strangled sound left me. She didn't go there. Not with Kira. Kira's brother Cameron Barron ran the refinery, and while he'd ruled his family with an iron fist, he'd been a well-liked and respected CEO. It didn't make sense, but it made him the best boss. Which Kira fucking hated.

Nora clicked her phone off and tossed it on the table. "I'm so over her temper tantrums."

"What'd you do? She might fire me."

Nora scoffed. Her phone began to ring. "She won't. Then she'd have to find someone who works as hard as you for the low pay I'm sure you're getting."

One of us was confident in my job security. "It's not low." Her phone kept ringing. I didn't have to look to see it was Kira.

Nora rolled her eyes. "It was probably low when she offered you the job. It's definitely shit pay now."

"It put my daughter through college." Which was more than I could've asked for when Kira first hired me.

"Sixteen years of wages should do a lot more than that, Colt." She propped her hands on her hips. A charge built in the air between us. We weren't in a standoff, we were in agreement, mostly, but I couldn't ignore how she defended me. How she didn't flinch when she'd learned of my homeless, jobless past.

The phone stopped, then started again. Nora ignored it.

"Look, you can defend her all you want," she said. "I get it. You made a ton of mistakes. You were homeless before she took a chance on you. But you're worth more. You were worth more then, and you deserve more now."

Shame swept through me, mingling with the panic. Yet...

I respected the hell out of few people in the world, and Nora was one of them. She spoke so frankly about my treatment. She spoke about me being homeless as if it was nothing more than a blip on the radar of life.

It had been a defining time in my life.

She said I deserved more with unquestioning conviction. And what if I did deserve more? If I kept ditching my daughter, seeing the disappointment in her eyes when I didn't know how to connect with a little baby who had a mop of hair the same color as mine, I'd lose what we'd built over the last sixteen years. I'd end up visiting less often. I worked so damn hard to see her when I finally got on my feet. I'd worked up to seeing her for a quick, supervised turnaround trip to taking a week for her college graduation to being a proud papa sitting next to the man who raised her. Meanwhile, I was planning to visit less. I'd already left early, embarrassed I had no clue what to do with a grandkid. I'd devolve back into nothing but being a name on a paycheck.

I might deserve more, but this job was all I had.

Yet...I wanted more. Just this once. I wanted to be more

than a dad with a troubled past who hardly ever visited. More than a grandpa who suffered his first bout of anxiety around a tiny baby. More than a hired guy to the strong, generous woman who had a thing for me when she could've landed anyone. More than a guy who wondered what it'd be like to have someone like her in his arms.

Nora's phone stopped and started again. She glowered at it, then at me, clear challenge in her eyes.

If I did this, there was no going back. I could be torching my job. I was risking the support I was sending my family. But Nora had defended me. She knew all of me and still she stood her ground at my side.

She could do so much fucking better than me, but I would be the one making sure she was taken care of. I marched to the table, picked up the phone, and answered it, "Kira. I've earned the right to be a grown man in this apartment that I've paid for in sweat equity. What Nora and I do is none of your business. If you want to fire me, I can't stop you. I'll take care of things until your plane touches down."

I clicked the phone off and tossed it on the table. This time, I was the one with the challenge in my eye. Heat licked up and down my spine. The door to my lust had been cracked open for days. Now it was flung wide. "Nora, I fucking want you."

Her lips parted. I had one heartbeat of doubt before she rounded the table and flung herself into me. I caught her, wrapped my arms around her waist to hug her tight, and slammed my mouth onto hers.

I never dared entertain ideas about what I'd do with Nora if I got her, but I would've thought slow and sensual. She was an expensive delicacy to be savored. But I planned to gobble her up. Savoring, lingering, all that would come later. After I knew what heaven felt like.

I lifted her and made it as far as the back of the couch.

Her ass hit the middle, and we stopped. She was tearing my shirt off as our tongues tangled.

"You're so damn sweet, just like I thought you'd be," I growled. "I'm gonna taste all of you."

She groaned. "Do you know how long I've waited to hear that?"

"What else have you waited for?"

"That beard between my legs."

My erection cut into my zipper so hard I saw stars. "Christ, baby. I don't think I'm going to make it that long. I need to get inside you."

She yanked my undershirt over my head. Her hands were at my waistband while I was yanking her leggings down. Each inch of skin that was bared kept me in stark disbelief. This was happening. I was giving in and taking something I wanted.

Her fingertips brushed the tip of my cock. I sucked my stomach in and had to take a breather. One light touch and I was done for.

Instead of backing off, she yanked her shirt off, then shoved my jeans down and fisted my dick.

"Jesus, angel."

She gave me a lazy pump, not knowing how close I was to exploding. "I like when you call me that."

"You're my snow angel." I lifted one of her legs to free it from a legging. She didn't let go of me, so I didn't bother with the other leg. The sight in front of me shorted my brain. Sexy. "Fuck."

"You didn't stare at my brownies like that."

I had to be inside her, but those pretty, wet, pink folds had to be explored. I dropped to my knees.

"But your couch—"

I silenced her with a look. Fuck the couch. Her thighs were on either side of my head and her soft, musky scent was close enough to taste. She bit her lower lip, and that was all I could take.

I descended on her, licking through her slit until her clit was mine to dominate. My body was tight, holding myself together long enough to pleasure her. I wasn't known for my finesse. I had sex like I did everything else. I was good, proficient, and I made sure my partner had no complaints.

But I thoroughly savored Nora. I enjoyed hearing her little pants, the way she'd tighten and shudder when I hit her clit just right. When she made those noises, I didn't feel like I wasn't good enough for her. In this, I could outdo whatever was required. I didn't free my hands from her thighs. I was dying to be inside her, but I couldn't have her toppling backward.

"Oh, god, Colt. Oh—" She went rigid for a heartbeat. Heat blasted my face, and she started riding my tongue. "Yes! Oh. My god. Yes!"

My ego had never inflated so big. Keeping a hold of her, I rose and positioned myself.

Her eyes were liquid, dreamy. She was panting, but she gripped my shoulders. My religious use of condoms had nearly been destroyed. Nora might want kids, but she'd think twice about having mine if she was smart. Hastily, I dug a condom out of my wallet and fumbled rolling it on while she stroked her hands over my chest and abdomen, her thighs clamped around me.

Finally, my cock was at her entrance, and we both watched as I slowly sank inside. Her body gripped me with a desperation that was much like my own. She moaned as I filled her. Hot and wet. Tight. Sweat dotted my forehead, and as soon as she experienced as deep as I could go, I withdrew and thrust. Her boobs bounced, and she arched.

Fucking heaven.

"Yes. More."

I did it again and cinched her to me. My strokes were short, hard, and her clit brushed against my lower abdomen. Her eyes went glassy, and she tightened around me. Hell yes. I was older than her, but I had experience on my side. I could fuck her brains out and make her come five times before midnight.

Gritting my teeth, I fought against my climax while experiencing intense pleasure I'd never known. The first quakes went through her body and right into my dick. She was close to coming again.

"Come for me, Nora." I pumped into her, our foreheads touching, both of us hyper focused on where we were connected. "Come all over me again."

She shattered, crying and shaking in my arms. The most beautiful damn sight I'd ever seen. I clenched my teeth against the power of my release. I spilled into her, her body milking mine until I was empty. Until I had nothing to give and was completely hers.

Aftershocks gripped and caressed my cock. I'd blown up my world for the best sex of my life. Reality couldn't penetrate my orgasmic haze.

"That was even better than I thought it'd be."

Damn right it was. I planted a kiss on her lips, and she amped it up, catching my lips between her teeth. Already, my cock was back on board.

This woman. I pulled out of her, loving how she watched and didn't try to hide herself.

"Wait here." I disposed of the condom in record time and went back to her and picked her up. Everything inside me clicked into place. She felt right.

She wrapped her arms around me and peered at the back of the couch. "We're going to need a spot treatment."

"Might as well wait until tomorrow. I've got plans for you."

A sexy grin spread across her face. "Promise?" She caught my cheeks in her hands. "Tell me you're not secretly freaking out? Are you pissed at yourself? Are you tucking me in and leaving to sleep in the cold house?"

She continued to worry about me. People all my life had left me alone to do my thing. I'd wanted them to. But Nora's concern was like the rest of her. I wasn't sure what I would do without her after experiencing her.

I tugged the covers back and set her down. She looked so fucking right in my bed. Even better when I knew I was crawling in with her. "I'm not leaving you, Nora." I pulled her shirt off and unhooked her bra. "You kicked the door wide open and showed me possibilities. Ones I can't quit thinking about. And we're going to have to have a talk about us and what this means." I flung the bra behind me. "But I can't think when you're naked."

Her gaze dropped to my proud erection. "Talking later works for me."

* * *

Nora

He was in me again. The man was an orgasm charmer. He could coax one out of nowhere with little more than his tongue or a fingertip. And when he used his gloriously thick cock? I was in heaven.

He moved over me. I had my legs wrapped around his waist as he powered in and out of me. He knew I was close, but since he'd already come, he was taking his time. My body was his, and he was using it.

The flex of his ass under my heels was perfection. The way he'd kiss my lips, then nuzzle my neck with his beard until I thought my body would shatter into a million plea-sure-filled pieces. It was more than I could've hoped for.

My thing for Colt paled to actually being with him. He was a deeper, more sensitive man than I could've ever imag-ined. He'd always done thoughtful things, but I had assumed they were out of a sense of duty, an obligation, a part of his responsible personality he couldn't control. But he'd been a man who held himself apart until it came to me.

He made me feel special, treasured, by being his real self.

"Colt," I whimpered, trailing my fingers over his many tattoos. I'd inspect and lick each one, commit them to memory. Another hidden part of him I hadn't known about. We were connected. We couldn't be any closer, but he was stroking in and out of my body, and I needed more.

"Tell me what you want, angel."

His endearments. I was a goner. "You know what I want."

He flashed a smile. Both of us were slicked with sweat, but we clung to each other. "I like to hear you say it."

"You. I need you to get me off in only the way you can." I lost my mind with him. All my insecurities. There was nothing but him and how good I felt.

"Like this?" He slid a hand between our bodies and cranked one of my legs up.

I was more open to him than ever. "Yes," I groaned.

Within seconds, I exploded again. He'd broken my "orgasms in a day" record as soon as he'd given me my second one. Three would just be untouchable. My body had already reserved every climax for him. "Colt!"

"That's it. Let me feel you come around me. That tight little pussy gripping me tight."

Another cry left me, and his thrust quickened. He shat-tered with me, both of us careening over the edge.

He didn't just roll off me but lavished me with long

kisses and sweet murmurings laced with swear words. Pure Colt.

"You're so fucking beautiful, Nora. I'll never get enough of you."

"Good thing I'm not limiting you."

A chuckle shook his body, and he smiled down at me. It was official. I perished in the storm and would exist only in this dream. When he pulled out of me, he kept me snuggled in his embrace. Sex with Colt had been a pipe dream. Cuddling? I was definitely no longer on this plane.

I didn't know what the future held for us. I only hoped that when the storm cleared, reality didn't destroy what we were building together.

Six

NORA

It was morning. The power was still out, but Colt's apartment was cozy. Even more intimate with him in the bed.

"Dude, like where did you get this mattress?" I rolled to my stomach and pulled the sheet away to look at the brand.

"Keep saying words like 'dude,' and my balls are going to wrinkle."

I rolled back over and tucked into his side. "Colt, your balls are too big to wrinkle."

He snorted out a laugh. "You've only gotten more shameless."

"Well, look who my mother is."

He chuckled and fell quiet.

I traced through his soft chest hair. We hadn't talked about Mom's calls. I didn't want her toxicity to intrude, but I wasn't her employee. I could just leave. For some reason, Colt acted like this job was his only chance.

"What will you do if she fires you?" I'd have to be gone by the time the wind died down and the interstate opened. Colt would take care of the cattle and let his work ethic persuade Mom to let him keep his job. She'd be calmer around just him. My presence was an incendiary device, and I couldn't have Colt getting punished for her anger toward me. I could see if the motel in town had a room open for the holiday weekend so I could celebrate with Holden and his family. Otherwise, I was driving to Bismarck to have Christmas alone.

"I'll pack my shit and look for a new job," he said after a few moments.

He'd never admit he was stressed. Sending money to his family was important to him, but I suspected he was more worried about looking like a deadbeat to them. About telling those he'd let down in a way he couldn't forgive himself for that he was jobless and homeless. He could get work again. He was a good employee, and any Barron other than Mom would vouch for him. But his pride was so strong. He didn't want them to think he was a failure.

He'd opened up to me, and I'd interfered. "I'm not sorry about what we did, but I'm sorry it disrupted your life. I'd feel awful if you have to move, but you'd have no problem getting a job. You have an entire town, hell, the county, who would be a reference for you. If there are no ranches needing help in the area, there might be work in Bismarck."

I was as stiff as an icicle next to him. Why'd I feel like I'd asked him to move in with me? He wasn't a city guy.

He twisted so we were on our sides, face-to-face. His soapy scent surrounded us. Sex permeated the air. We'd had enough of it. He'd outperformed any guy I'd been with, but I wasn't surprised. I was quite delighted he'd surpassed my fantasies.

"Bismarck?" he asked.

"Yeah. I mean, it's an option." An option where he'd be with me all the time. I liked the sound of that, but I wasn't sure what he'd think.

His lips formed a troubled line. "What if I don't get fired? Would you consider moving back to Coal Haven?"

I opened my mouth. Closed it again. Would I? Coal Haven would never cease being my home in my mind, but the town wasn't where I'd built a life. Yet, I never thought I'd have a shot with Colt. "I don't know. You're here, so that's a major factor." How much of myself would I sacrifice to be with him? Would I have to give up a thing? "When I ran the farmers' market for Uncle Cameron, I was firmly under the Barron umbrella. Nothing I said mattered. Only what he said. I like the freedom of Bismarck. But this is new, and oh god, I was basically asking you to move in when your life might be upended because of me. And then I wrote off coming back home permanently right away. I'm selfish, just like Mom has said—"

"Nora."

Insecurity draped over me like another blanket. "Sorry. I'm moving way too fast. Forget I said—"

He put a finger over my lips, and I flicked my tongue out. His gaze darkened, but he slid the finger down my neck to my chest and circled my nipple. I shuddered. I had beard burn between my thighs, across my chest, along my neck, and on my stomach.

It'd been a busy night of climaxing.

"We're adjusting," he said. "We went from a glacial pace to talking about moving, but the last five years, I've barely seen you." He nipped the pearled tip of my nipple. "And I wanted to."

"Only for five years?"

"You would've been twenty-five," he said, sounding incredulous.

I arched a brow. I was messing with him, but a pleasant energy buzzed under my skin. He'd been into...me! He'd fought it for so many years, and maybe I should be insulted, but I wore it like a badge of honor.

"Okay, seven years, but that made you twenty-three, which is *not* better."

"Seven years? What suddenly changed?" Other than my looks and my confidence from living on my own away from home and being in charge of my health and nutrition.

"I saw you as a woman, for one. I couldn't miss it." He traced a finger over my lips. "That was the first time your smile sucker punched me right in the nuts. Then seeing your ass did other things to my nuts."

Seven years we'd missed, but we weren't in the free and clear. There was my mom. His daughter. I knew all about family considerations when it came to personal decisions, but I had to know if there were more reasons. I finally dug into Colt, but there were layers to him—to my delight. "So, seven years, we ignored what turned out to be mutual attraction. Other than my age or last name, what made you wait?"

A muscle jumped in his jaw, but I recognized the look in his eye. He got that ashamed glint when he was thinking about his past.

"I've never had my own place," he admitted. "I thought this was it, but as you pointed out, it's not."

If he hadn't melted my heart with each earth-shattering orgasm, his confession would've done it. "Never?"

He shook his head. "I was kicked out at sixteen. I bounced from couch to couch, getting the boot when a girlfriend, friend, or family member got sick of my shit. Then I roamed. If I needed cash, I'd do an odd job, I'd take some work, but I was never good for long."

"Drugs? Alcohol?"

He shrugged. "Yes. Thank fuck I never progressed

beyond recreational. Mostly, I was getting into fights. Speeding. Crashing cars. Stupid, pointless shit, Nora. When your mom found me, I was stranded in a small town in the middle of Montana. She was transporting a new horse she bought."

"And promptly sold." Mom had shiny object syndrome when it came to horses. She'd held on to mine and Holden's, surprisingly, but she went through mounts like they were trading cards and none of them valuable.

"Yep. Porterhouse. Remember him?"

"He was a mean bastard."

He grinned. "He gave her hell that drive. She'd had him out of the trailer to water him, and he blew up and got away from her."

I grinned, picturing it in my head. Mom swearing up a storm. Colt calmly moving in and catching Porterhouse. "Surprised she didn't take him straight to a kill corral after that."

"Your mom likes the ornery ones."

Made sense. "So did she just offer you a job?"

"Sort of. She asked where I learned to handle a horse like that."

"And?"

"I said I had less to lose than the horse."

A simple answer Mom would respect. If Colt had reached the point where he took accountability for himself, she'd be hooked. "Are you sure she wasn't trying to pick you up?"

He arched a dark brow. "Have you seen the men your mom dates?"

"I try not to."

"She likes the business guys, snow angel. Haven't you ever noticed?"

Thinking about my mom's taste in men was weird. I

usually felt bad for the guy, but at the same time, it wasn't like she hid who she was. Mom's sense of self was strong and unashamed. Some of her dates thought they could change her, or they thought they liked a strong woman. They were wrong on both accounts. "Holden's dad is a lawyer. Mine is in sales. Oh. My. God. How did I never notice?"

"The suits are like catnip to her."

I made a gagging sound. "Stop it."

"They think they can tame her." His grin was pure wicked. "But I'm sure that doesn't extend to bed."

"Grooooosss, Colt." I rolled to my back, laughing.

He smirked. "She said she knew you were into me, and that's why you dated pussies."

Mortified at Mom's accurate observation and that she told Colt, I groaned and flung an arm over my face. She never gave me a hard time about it. So unlike her. Probably because I did date the opposite of Colt, and nothing would stick. Those guys weren't Colt, and that meant I'd stay single, which she preferred for some reason.

He whipped the covers off. "We gotta feed the cattle and check the power. But first..." He slid down my body, shoving my thighs open as he went. Desire flooded my veins, an endless supply when it came to him.

"Again? Already?"

He looked up, his mouth hovering right above my sex. "When it comes to you, it'll always be again and already."

* * *

Colt

I leaned against the shop counter and read the message. Nora was outside moving snow, and I didn't have to worry about her seeing. Kira had given up on blasting my phone and Nora's with missed calls. Her texts to each of us were **Answer your fucking phone** and nothing more.

The power was on, but Nora stayed with me. She'd packed all the luggage she'd brought from Bismarck and stowed her belongings in my apartment. What she didn't worry would freeze was in her car. Kira would be home after Christmas, and Nora wanted to be gone before then.

We hadn't talked about what happened after Christmas. The holding pattern was necessary until I knew whether I had a job. I just wasn't sure how long she'd want me after she went back to the city and her business.

And if I had a job, then...what would we do? Long distance? As long as she wanted me, I was hers.

I was used to being alone. I wasn't used to being alone after being with Nora.

Another message pinged. I impassively read it, expecting another *Answer your fucking phone* from Kira. The message was from Brittany. **I really wish you could've stayed longer.**

My initial pleased surprise turned to dismay, sinking my stomach with it. I had planned for two weeks with Brittany and her family, and I'd barely made it a week.

I wanted to see her again. When she'd handed me Berkley, my heart had nearly thudded out of my chest. I wasn't a baby holder. I hadn't cradled Brittany or given her a damn bottle. I'd heard guys boast about never changing a diaper, but not me. Shame was a permanent mark on my skin for not having changed one diaper.

I had a second chance, and I risked fucking it up. Maybe I would rock a baby. Cradle Berkley. Give her a bottle.

The image of Nora smiling at me over a tiny bundle in her arms made me damn near burst. What if I could do it again and not fail?

If she wanted me to give up this job and move to the city, would I? I wasn't above honest pay of any kind. I could stock shelves, mop floors, or drive a delivery van. Honorable work with good paychecks.

But I'd miss the outdoors. I'd miss hearing the cows lowing in the morning and at night. I'd miss the croak of the frogs, the noisy birds, and the sound of the wind flowing over the shop.

I loved being a cowboy. But I was falling in love with Nora more. Once she broke down my walls, I was a goner.

Nora entered the shop, stomping snow off her boots. She'd been driving the tractor with the new snowblower attachment, clearing the rest of the driveway. She was a precision expert in that thing and strategically piled the snow to minimize blowing and drifting. Even better, she enjoyed it, and I'd gotten to watch her grin and plow.

When she saw me, concern infused her eyes. "What's wrong?"

"Nothing. Brittany just said she wished I didn't have to go so soon." I hadn't regretted leaving early until now. The irony that I wouldn't have had this time with Nora wasn't lost on me. Was the universe telling me I couldn't have both a family and a good woman?

She took off her hat, leaving golden-brown hair plastered to her head. Her cheeks were red from the wind and cold. I would fill them with a different sort of flush later. "What made you leave early? You said you felt unneeded."

I sounded whiny when she put it like that. "We were out to eat with her parents, and they were passing Berkley around." I couldn't bring myself to say the rest. Fucking embarrassing.

Her eyes went liquid. "Did you panic?"

The tension around my chest loosened. No judgment was in her tone. "Damn near." I stared at my screen. "My granddaughter is the first baby I've ever held. She started crying, and I had no fucking clue what to do."

"Who would if they'd never been around babies?"

"I have a kid, Nora." I should've been around a baby, which was the problem. I shouldn't be an ignorant fuck about kids when I was a dad. "Yet Berkley was the first baby I've held."

"Yeah," she said like *duh*. "And you've owned your behavior. So move on and learn what to do with your granddaughter. It's okay to have to get taught. You weren't born knowing how to pull calves."

I'd been through some harrowing calving seasons. The first time I'd watched an old rancher put chains on a calf inside the mama, I'd thought about how I wanted to be a badass like him. And I'd done it.

The calves were my job. But I'd learned. I could approach being a grandpa with the same sense of responsibility. Nora was right. "You're fucking amazing, you know it?"

"I won't get tired of hearing it." She beamed and unzipped her coat. "What if you went back?"

"To Idaho?"

"Once the roads are open, head back. Tell Mom you're taking a few more days. She'll be here, and if she doesn't fire you, she owes you. You've been working for the last four days. You could get there in time for Christmas."

"I can't invite myself for Christmas." Unfamiliar anxiety filled my chest. I'd never spent a holiday with Brittany. Those days were for her family, the ones who'd been around for her. They'd earned her time. I went for big life events, like graduation, or just because during the autumn after we worked cattle.

Nora crossed to me, smelling like cold sunshine and fresh snow overlaid with exhaust from the tractor. "Call her anyway." She sauntered into the apartment like she knew I needed privacy. Because she was a fucking goddess.

If I called Brittany, I'd have to tell her I fell hard for a woman not much older than her. I might even feel the urge to confess how long I'd been denying my attraction to Nora. I'd definitely have to admit that she was my boss's daughter. I'd rather have an honest conversation than have my daughter feel like I was hiding my relationship from her. I'd learned a long time ago an honest life was the only way I could live.

Nora wasn't a mistake. There was nothing to hide. Being with her was like getting a taste of a life I wasn't meant to have. Not quite forbidden, but decadent. Expensive. And I was a broke man.

The buzz of a snowmobile sounded outside.

Ah, fuck. It could only be one person, and I hadn't even factored him into the whole process of seeing Nora.

The shop door yanked open, and Holden stepped in. He stopped when his eyes adjusted to the dimmer interior, and he saw me leaning against the workbench. He took his snow-studded hat off and hit it against his leg, raining chunks of snow onto the ground. I braced myself for the confrontation. Would Holden forget about our history and act like I was the worst thing that could happen to his sister? Would he give me a chance to prove I wasn't? Losing his friendship would hurt, but after Nora's stanch defense, I wasn't settling for less from him.

"So," he said and crossed his arms.

"Your mom called you."

"Yep. She had a lot to say."

I faced the man who'd treated me like a friend from the first day we met. Holden had accepted me into his life, he'd taught me a shitload about ranching when I thought I knew it all, and he'd brought me into his fold. He and his cousin

Stetson would be like brothers to me if I knew what having brothers was like.

My throat grew tight. Holden should've heard the news from me. I should've called him this morning when I could finally pry myself off Nora. "Me and Nora..."

He tapped his gloved fingers, waiting. How did I explain to the man I wanted his sister like I'd never wanted anything in my life? That I'd tasted her, and there would be no going back? I didn't. He was her brother.

"You and Nora?" he prompted.

"She's, uh..." Someone I was willing to give up a stable job for? She was also the one who pointed out this job wasn't exactly stable, and my boss liked having her thumb on my life.

"I can tell you what she's not." Holden's voice was hard. "She's not someone you just fuck when you feel like it. She's not the type of girl who's just going to go on her way when you tell her that you're a one-and-done guy." Now probably wasn't the time to tell him we were way beyond one time. "And if you think you're suddenly in love and that you can actually commit to something more than waking up each day, doing ranch shit, and picking up girls at the bar, she's not the type of girl who should be pulled back to this town to live with a selfish mom. Nora got out. She's doing well for herself. Are you fucking with her?"

Anger licked up the back of my neck. "I'm not fucking with her."

"Colt, you're a good guy," he said with less simmering anger. "But I know what you're like with women."

An irritated flush crept up my face. "And what were you like with women before you met Emery?"

His lips formed a hard line. "That was different."

"How? Nora's not much younger than Emery was when you met her. Nora's not much younger than *you* were. And

I'm not dragging her away from her successful coffee shop. I might even end up in Bismarck." My voice was raw saying it.

He stared at me like we'd never met, and I'd just told him his past, present, and future. "You're quitting?"

I would to be with Nora. She had faith in me, and sometimes a guy's gotta have more of that in his life. "If your mom fires me."

He crossed his arms, the material of his jacket crackling from being cold. "So, you're not leaving?"

"Pretty sure I'll get fired. Kira's pretty pissed."

"She said you and Nora are shacking up."

I wished, but I'd rather have Kira understand how I felt about her daughter. Maybe she did know, and it pissed her off. "Nora stayed here while the power was out. I tried to be honorable, I swear."

"Meaning you haven't been honorable?"

"Your sister has a way of getting what she wants." I folded my arms. Nora had said to own it, and she was right again. I wasn't hiding how I felt about her. "And I want to make her happy."

He chuffed. "She's wanted you for long enough."

"I tried not to notice her. I wasn't attracted to her until she was living here for a while after she was done with college, and then...she would've been all I noticed if I didn't lock away how she made me feel."

He considered me. "You and Mom never..."

"Fuck no." My stomach twisted. I grimaced. "Do I have to have the talk with you about how your mom likes guys with suits and money?"

"Please don't. I'm already queasy thinking about you and Nora."

We were moving back into our normal easiness. "I know I'm a piece of shit—"

"Not what I said."

I shrugged. "I was."

"We all wish we were different when we were younger. Better. Smarter. Braver." He took his gloves off and rubbed a spot between his eyes. "Is she different?"

"Yes," I said roughly.

"Emery was different from the moment I met her."

"I couldn't tell," I said wryly. He'd been morose when he thought he wasn't going to see her after she fled their backseat hookup. Good thing he ended up being her son's football coach and being persistent as fuck.

He smirked. "I'm talking about before we— Yuck. I do not want to think of you and my sister."

"She's..." I rubbed the back of my neck. "Look, when she moved home after college, and I couldn't not notice her, I knew she was too good for me. She wasn't even an option in my head. I might as well try to fly to the moon before I could date her. And then she was coming into money when she turned twenty-five, and she wouldn't tell anyone, but I knew she had big plans. She didn't need a guy like me dragging her down."

"And you don't think you will now?" He was curious, not accusatory.

Nora was why it was so important I didn't start something with her and then become homeless and jobless. "There's no world in existence where she's not better than me."

His brows rose. "Well. I don't know your history—"

"My daughter's two years younger than her. Full disclosure."

He stared, his eyes growing incrementally wider. "What the hell? You have a *kid*? You're a *dad*?"

"I was a sperm donor. I didn't do nothin' for her until Kira hired me. Then she got every cent I didn't need. Now it goes to my granddaughter." Well. That was out. I wasn't hiding my family anymore either. I'd keep working to make them proud of me.

His eyes flared even more. "You have a granddaughter too? Shit, Colt. What else don't I know?"

He almost sounded offended. Insulted that I hadn't trusted him with the truth, and for the first time, I regretted not telling him sooner. He was the closest friend I had, and I should've treated him like it. "She wasn't the secret. How absent I was from her life was what I didn't care to share. Same with the years before your mom hired me when I was a good-for-nothing with no roof over my head."

More surprise rippled over his face. He nodded, understanding traveling over his features. "I see where you're coming from."

The door to my apartment opened, and Nora peeked her head out. Her hair framed her face, and she was so goddamn lovely. She studied her brother, likely determining his reaction to us, but unsurprised he was here. "I thought I heard more than one guy talking." She waved us in. "We've got leftover brownies."

Panic danced across Holden's face.

"They're actually good," I muttered to Holden, and he coughed to hide a laugh.

She narrowed her eyes at me. "I heard that. I'll give you a spanking tonight."

Holden choked, sputtering, and I couldn't help but chuckle at his discomfort—otherwise I would've died she'd said that around him. I clapped him on the shoulder. "She's kidding."

"Am I?" Nora disappeared into the apartment, leaving the door open for us.

Holden's acceptance meant a lot. I'd have to talk to my daughter and then it'd just be waiting for Kira's reaction. But the talk with Holden had brought up a good point. If

Kira didn't fire me, was I brave enough to leave everything I knew, the only steady paycheck I'd had as an adult, and risk being a stone tied to Nora's ankle?

* * *

Nora

Holden stayed for a snack before he had to run home to finish moving snow at his place. My brother had left, but Colt's pensive energy stayed. Since Holden had eyed us like he couldn't believe what he was seeing but didn't interrogate me, I assumed he and Colt had come to an understanding. So, the only other topics that could bother Colt that much were me, my mom, or his daughter. He'd mentioned he hadn't called her yet, but he would.

Colt was washing dishes. Mom wouldn't spring for a dishwasher, but Colt probably used very few dishes every day.

I finished wiping the table, then clicked through my phone until I pulled up the North Dakota road map. The sun had been out all day and the wind had died down. "The roads are open to the Montana border now. They have scattered ice, but they'll clear by tomorrow."

He grabbed a dish towel and gave me a knowing look. "Your mom's not home yet."

The anticipation was killing me. I hated confrontations with Mom, and this was building into a doozy.

The shop door squeaked open, louder because of the open space, and I stared at the apartment door, my pulse pounding.

"Who would that be?" I asked. Holden had already

stopped by. Mom wouldn't arrive this quickly. Who else could she have sicced on us?

A steady thud of boots echoed from the interior of the shop. No wonder Colt knew whenever someone entered. There was no soundproofing when it came to the inside of the building.

Someone knocked. "It's me."

My stomach sank right to my feet. Uncle Cameron. Mom went straight to the top. Cameron's word had been law for so long. He'd changed over the years, softened, but I didn't want to find out if he could be the old Cameron again.

"I'll get it." Colt set the dish towel down and opened the door for our unexpected guest.

Uncle Cameron stepped in, his eyes narrowed, lines winging out from the corners. Gray dusted through his hair, but he was tall and broad-shouldered like my brother and my guy cousins.

"Nora. What a surprise." His tone was so dry I couldn't parse amusement from it. I had thought my uncle would barge in, put Colt in his place with a few denigrating words, and order me to the house, expecting complete compliance. I wouldn't have obeyed, but my body quivered, ready for the challenge.

"Seems to be for some," I said.

"And not a surprise to others?" he asked mildly.

Colt and I exchanged a look. He was guarded. I was growing confused.

"What others?" I asked. Mom had been plenty shocked. Holden had apparently known I had a thing for Colt, but when the wind lessened, he'd still rushed over to drill into Colt.

"Have a seat." Colt pulled out a chair at the table, then slid into his spot.

Cameron held a hand up. "I won't be staying long. You two are adults, and Nora's not in danger."

Colt's brows drew together in a troubled line. "I'd never hurt her."

"I know." The corner of his mouth tipped up, and he eyed Colt. "It's you I should be worried about. Been dealing with Barron women my entire life." He clicked his tongue and glanced between us. Was Colt like me and didn't know what the hell to do? "Well, I can tell my sister to settle the hell down."

"She'll totally listen," I said.

He flashed a quick grin but sobered. He put his hand on the doorknob and paused. "My generation of Barrons tend to be our own worst enemy. That's definitely true in Kira's case, and I don't know that she'll get the wake-up call I got. I hope not, but that means she'll keep being a stubborn cuss out for blood."

The worst-kept family secret was Uncle Cameron's chronic leukemia. His case was well managed, but between his illness and how he'd almost lost touch with his kids, he'd changed.

I wasn't sure losing me would do it for Mom, and she'd keep Colt around just to keep him away from me. With his pride and need to prove himself, I wasn't sure he'd break away to be with me.

Seven

COLT

I was sitting on the edge of the bed, phone to my ear, staring at the floor while Nora showered. After Cameron's visit last night, we'd done evening chores and read until I hauled her across the couch and on my lap for a ride.

"Thanks for telling me, Colt." Baby noises punctuated Brittany's words. It had never bothered me that she referred to me by name and called her stepdad dad. If anything, I would've felt more like a pile of shit. "I can't wait to meet her. We can talk about clothes and paint our nails and do each other's hair." She pitched her voice up. She had a wicked sense of humor.

"Smart-ass," I said with loads of affection oozing out.

"I'm told I get that from you. When do you think you'll get a chance to come out again? Dad wanted to catch you for some cattle talk."

If I had been a better person, I might've met the man who married Brittany's mom and raised my daughter, and we'd have become fast friends. But when I went to Idaho, I tried not to interfere with their family time. "I'm not sure when I'll get away."

"Are you waiting until Nora can come too?" She sounded hopeful. I couldn't have asked for a better kid.

"It's work keeping me here." Acid burned up my throat with the almost lie.

"Oh." Her disappointment gutted me. "Well, we're all just hanging out at my house until the end of the year. Ben banked enough leave, and you're welcome any time. Even if it's Christmas Day."

Her offer was as genuine as it'd always been, but this was the first time I didn't brush her off. "I'll let you know. Love ya, Brittany."

"Bye, Colt."

Nora's words ran through my head. I was owed time off, but I hadn't missed a day that wasn't planned and permitted in advance since I started. Taking vacation was almost painful, but I'd done it for Brittany. Less than a week ago, I'd cut loose early for bullshit reasons. I was letting my daughter down again.

I was still staring at the floor when Nora came out of the bathroom dressed in a red-and-green Christmas sweater I hadn't seen before. She was squeezing dampness out of her hair with a navy-blue towel. "How'd it go?"

I hadn't told her I was going to call my daughter. I hadn't planned on it. I had a moment and just did it, but Nora was perceptive. "She's cool. Wants me to go out there before the end of the year."

"Good." She stepped back into the bathroom to hang the towel up. My place had never smelled so good. Her shampoo permeated the air like a thousand bouquets of flowers were strewn about. "Are you?"

"We'll see how things settle here." I had a hard time

coming to terms with visiting Idaho when I was unemployed. If I needed to stay and smooth things over, I would and I'd figure out the vacation situation later.

She gave a resolute nod. She didn't agree with my determination not to torch my job, but she respected my wishes.

I needed to hang on to this girl. She challenged me, but she didn't let our differences or the fact that I made her wait seven years before making a move on her change her position in the relationship. In her mind, we were equals. In my mind, she was so far above me I'd never reach her. But I was a stubborn man and a starving one who would never get enough of Nora Barron.

She went to the kitchen. "Want to watch a movie? I can make some popcorn."

I warily eyed her. "What would you put on the popcorn?"

"Scaredy-cat?"

"I'm not leaving this world because I choked on a dry kernel."

Laughing, she said, "Butter, smart-ass. I don't drink straight milk anymore, but I have a love affair with butter."

"Want help?"

"No, pick out the movie and surprise me."

Nora liked slapstick comedy, and I liked my movies like I liked my books—dark, gritty, and with extra intrigue. Since she was reading my books, I picked out an oldie but a goodie. *Conspiracy Theory*. The noise of popping filled the air. I had the movie ready by the time the savory smell of popcorn reached my nose.

She sat next to me, a big bowl balanced between us. This was domestic bliss. My woman. Popcorn and a movie. Chores were done. Snow was moved. The only thing that'd make it better was to have a Christmas tree in the corner. Holden used to make Christmas special for

Nora. When he'd moved away for college, he had relented. He and Emery made sure Nora had Christmas plans and was never sitting alone in Bismarck. Fuck if Kira would do that.

I was on the same level as Kira when it came to holidays. I didn't go out of my way to decorate or celebrate. Unlike her, I didn't go on a beach vacation either. I worked so she could leave town. I was usually invited to another Barron's place, and sometimes I stopped in to eat and took off to come read or watch a movie.

I'd be more like Holden from now on. Make it a day worthy for Nora to celebrate.

I was thinking long-term when it came to her.

The credits were rolling on the movie when the outside door to the shop slammed shut, shaking the building. My pulse jumped just as my stomach dropped.

Nora swung her wide gaze to me. We'd had a couple of surprise visitors, but they hadn't shut the door like it personally swindled their savings. "She wouldn't have come home early?"

My apartment door burst open. I peered over the back of the couch. A freshly tanned Kira stood in the doorway, her expression irate, her chest heaving. She wasn't wearing a coat heavy enough for the weather. She was in a light pullover and jeans, like she'd walked out of the hotel, to the airport, and came straight here, throwing on any extra clothing left in her pickup.

"Isn't this cute? You're playing house with my goddamn daughter." She propped her hands on her hips. "Care to explain why my employee and my daughter don't answer their fucking phones?"

"You were pissed," I answered. It was the truth. There was no other explanation. Resigned, I rose and rounded the couch, hoping to block Nora from the onslaught.

She flung her hands out. "Ya think? My goddamn kid, Colt."

"I'm an adult, Mom." Nora came to stand next to me, a united front, but her gut probably wasn't churning like mine. "You haven't made decisions for me in a long time."

She stabbed her finger toward Nora. "You use that excuse while you're staying in my house, eating my food?"

Nora stiffened. "You have no food to eat. And I'm helping take care of the animals. As I've already explained, you won't have to worry about me coming here again. I'm done with Coal Haven, and I'm done with you."

I inwardly winced at the Coal Haven part. I was determined to rescue my job. So what did that mean?

An emotion flickered in Kira's eyes. Hurt? Fear? "You're walking away from your family for a homeless man who abandoned his kid?"

The blow landed below the belt like she'd intended. Kira had kept my private life just that until she could use it against me. I was used to a lot of attitude from my boss, but she made this personal. I'd been nothing but an exemplary employee for over sixteen years, and the first time I cross her, she tosses my past in my face?

I did that well enough on my own.

"We all know that's bullshit, Mom," Nora said, taking a step. I put a quelling hand on her elbow. Kira had never hit her kids as far as I knew, but they were traversing new territory. "You can't admit you were wrong about me and him, and you want him at your beck and call because he's the only person in Coal Haven who'll take your shit and not leave."

Kira's brows rose, but her tan skin lost color. "Nora, you've always been a spoiled little—"

"That'll be enough," I said, stepping in front of Nora.

"Kira, you've said enough hurtful things to her. I'm not putting up with more."

Kira drew back. Her jaw was granite, and her light brown eyes flashed. She straightened, lifting her chin, resolve filling her gaze. I steeled myself, ready for the physical punch of the words coming my way.

"She said she was done with Coal Haven, Colt. Where does that leave you? Not a lot of ranches around Bismarck looking to hire a full-time employee. You gonna go work a cash register?"

She wasn't firing me. She also probably knew I didn't have savings. No nest egg. I was stuck unless I quit and moved in with Nora, if she'd have me. The idea of being jobless in a condo wasn't as repellent as it used to be only days ago.

What Kira's comment revealed was that Nora was right. This job, my wages, were a form of control. I was the only person on earth Kira could push around. She was controlling, and I was one of the few people in her life who gave her that sense of control. I was the constant in the storm of her life.

When I gave in to my feelings for Nora, it only reminded Kira of how powerless she really was. Holden supported me and Nora. Cameron. Their backing meant a lot. Their approval meant I wasn't a piece of shit. All the other Barrons likely didn't care either. As long as Nora was happy.

I'd never be happy with Nora if I stayed working for her mother. "I'll pack my things and leave, then."

Kira recoiled. "What?"

Nora's wide gaze burned into me. She slid her hand into mine and squeezed. I returned her touch. I'd been too afraid to walk away before, feeling like I had nothing and could give nothing. This week has been eye-opening.

"I quit," I said firmly.

Kira sneered, but the emotion from earlier was back in her gaze. Fear. "Relying on my daughter to support you?"

"It's a concern," I admitted. I was now jobless and homeless, but it was because I was standing up for myself and not giving up on me. "I've got a stash to get by for a while." Not long. "But first, I'd like to introduce her to my daughter and my grandkid."

Nora smiled. "Really?"

I nodded. Nora built me up. Kira kept her boot on me. Not a hard decision to know who was better for me. "I just need to pack first."

"You can't quit." A thread of panic wound around Kira's words.

"I just did." Inside, I was calmer than I thought I'd be. Losing this job used to be my worst nightmare, the signal I was delving back into a world I almost didn't make it out of. I might not have had faith in myself, but the girl at my side did. "The driveway's cleared. The cattle are doing fine. There were no issues with the horses. We're leaving the place in good shape. I'll ask Holden to store my bed. The rest will fit into my pickup." I drew Nora's hand to my mouth and kissed her knuckles.

She smiled and leaned against me. In her expression I saw pride, and goddamn if that didn't make me puff my chest out. "We'll be out of your life soon enough, Mom. I'm already packed."

The incredulous look Kira shot her was almost laughable. Didn't she know her own daughter yet? Of course, Nora was packed and ready to ditch this place. The girl was just as stubborn as her mom, but she wasn't mean about it. Nora's personality didn't emerge out of a place of defensiveness like her mother.

"It's gonna be Christmas," Kira said, sounding wooden.

Nora's fingers tightened. "Good thing you never went

out of your way to spend the holidays with me. Now, if you'll give us a few moments, we'll get out of your hair."

Kira's gaze jumped between us, her expression closing off and her jaw hardening. Finally, she spun on a boot heel and stormed out, slamming the door behind her. The strikes of her footsteps echoed through the shop until the exterior door was slammed as well.

Nora turned to face me, worry and regret lining her face. "I'm sorry. I came home for Christmas and made your life a mess."

I brushed my lips over her fingers once again. "You didn't make it a mess. It's wide open. Ready to meet my daughter?"

* * *

Nora

The road trip with Colt was uneventful but one of the best times of my life. The guy was even more talkative and open than I could've imagined.

As we took I-94 through Montana, he talked like he was trying to keep me from sinking into the last conversation with Mom. I was done with her, but at the same time, I couldn't believe she was out of my life. She'd go out of her way to avoid me at family gatherings, and I wouldn't talk to her. All my longings for a supportive mother were just... done.

But at the same time, I had a future with Colt to look forward to. Someone who had my back and faced his biggest fear for me and also for himself.

I soaked in everything he told me. He pointed in the direction of ranches where he'd worked for a hot minute.

He told me about being part of the crews that would drive cattle over long distances. He'd saved his money and then lived off the fumes when he crashed into town, loitering at gas stations and parking lots until another job came his way.

When we reached Idaho, he directed me to his daughter's place. She'd married a rancher and lived outside of Idaho Falls on a cute little spread with cattle, goats, and ponies.

Brittany had dark hair and brown eyes like Colt, only she was shorter than me, was unafraid to show emotion, and had a ready smile. I'd made a new friend.

Brittany poked at logs in the fireplace and set the poker down. Berkley was snoozing in a bassinet under the big picture window of the main room of the house. Colt was out with her husband, Ben, doing chores. They seemed to get along well.

"Colt's never been this relaxed before." She sat in the recliner next to me and tucked her feet under her. "He usually paces like he's got one foot out the door."

"He wasn't that different at home." I'd never quit thinking of Mom's place as home, but saying the word now left a pit of longing. I should've been over wishing things were different with her, but continuous rejection from a parent stuck with a girl. "I think he's only now given himself some forgiveness."

"And I think you're the reason why."

"No." I brushed her off, but she lifted a dark brow, saying so much with a few facial movements like her dad. "Maybe a little, but he was really upset with himself for leaving early, for feeling like he let you down again."

"I was a little let down," she murmured. "You know how you always want the approval of the parent who seems least willing to give it?"

Did I ever? "Unfortunately, yes. Except I never cared

about knowing my dad. My mom was enough of a challenge."

"Colt never talked about her. I assumed they had a thing together. I never would've thought..." Her lips quirked as she bit the inside of her cheek.

"Never would've thought he would have a thing for her daughter instead." I grinned. The situation was weird. There was zero chemistry between Mom and Colt. I had thought my attraction was one-sided, but he proved he and I had explosive chemistry. "Me either. Most of my life, my crush on him felt like a little girl idolizing a celebrity. I wasn't on his radar."

"Until you were?"

"I guess? He said he ignored it for years." I shrugged and gripped my coffee mug. I'd made my own blend for Brittany, and she made me set up a running order for her through my coffee shop. "I suppose the timing was right. I don't know if he'd have been in a place to risk his job." Plus, if he had acted on his feelings earlier, people would've said he was after my money, and his pride wouldn't have tolerated it.

"He sends me so much I asked him once if he was allergic to money." She directed her gaze toward the bassinet. "I'd rather have him around than get a paycheck. Berkley will be set for college before she's ten, but I hope Colt will keep visiting."

"He will." I didn't have to check with him to know he'd make sure he was present for his family.

The door opened on the lower level and sounds of cold, rustling winter gear preceded the guys piling in.

I craned my head around to watch Colt come up the stairs. The collar of his red flannel shirt was flipped up, and his cheeks were reddened above his beard. His gaze hit mine, heated, then slid to his daughter. The way he looked at Brittany and his grandbaby sent my hormones into a somersault.

He probably didn't know how much love shone from his face when he watched his family just living, but I noticed, and it got to me. The way he reacted dug down deep until I had the urge to throw out every condom he had—and we'd purchased a huge box on the trip.

Ben went to his wife, and Colt crossed to me. Brittany and I each got a kiss from our man, and not for the first time, I marveled over the way my Christmas vacation was turning out. We were heading back to North Dakota on Christmas Eve. Brittany's mom had invited us to her place, but Colt didn't want me missing out on Christmas with Holden and his family. I'd called him once we hit the road. Mom hadn't talked to him yet. She might've thought we were bluffing and was waiting for us to come back.

"Got a minute?" Colt held his hand out. I slipped mine into his, and he nodded at his daughter's questioning gaze. "It's nothing," he assured her.

He led me to the kitchen and dug out his phone.

On the screen was a message from Stetson. **Hear you might be looking for work?**

My gaze shot to Colt's. "He's offering you a job?"

"Looks like it." The phone slipped back into his shirt pocket.

"How would that work with Mom?"

"Stetson and Cameron would tell her to butt out. I'm more concerned with how it'd work between us."

Oh. He'd be working in Coal Haven with my family. My work was in Bismarck. Yet his main concern was us. This guy. "It'd only be an hour between us."

He pressed his hand flat on the counter and loosely propped his other hand on his hip. "I didn't miss out on years with you just so we can *not* see each other."

I stroked my hand along his cheek. The cool, silky texture of his beard ran under my skin. "That's sweet, but working for Stetson would be a good job. He's got two kids, and I'm sure he'd appreciate the help. He'll also treat you well."

"And where would you be?"

In my own place, free from my family's influence. "I would be..." Living in another town. He couldn't be the only one sacrificing. "I can commute. It's only an hour."

"Two hours a day? No. I'll tell him I have to pass."

"Colt, you can't do that. You have a family you want to take care of." I was the only one who had no one. My throat wanted to close up. I had my extended family, but losing Mom hit me harder than I could've imagined.

"And I'm gonna be taking care of you too, angel."

When he said that, I envisioned myself in a flowing white gown, ethereal and beautiful. Instead, I was a normal girl who wore an ugly Christmas sweater every day the week before Christmas. The one I had on today was the plainest green with plaid presents sewn all over and a red bow tied at the collar. It was hideous and one of my favorites. I even paired it with leggings that matched Colt's flannel.

Brittany had chortled and said "Matchies" when we arrived from the motel this morning. That was when I knew she and I would have no issues getting along.

"I'm doing fine. I have some left over from the trust." I'd saved a portion to live off of. I made smart choices with my car and my housing in case the coffee shop tanked and took my inheritance with it.

"I'm not talking about money, Nora."

He'd already lost his job because of me. I couldn't cost him another opportunity. Working with Stetson, and by some extension, Uncle Cameron, would be a good job. Colt would get compensated fairly, and he'd be able to get his own place.

If he moved to Bismarck, his options would be limited.

If he moved to Bismarck, it'd be a sign my roots were spreading in a town that didn't feel like home. The city was nice enough, but my condo was a base. I barely had enough room in the small yard to grow a few tomatoes and pepper plants. I had a bucket with potatoes, and my neighbor had commented about the ugly flowers.

"I know," I finally said. "Maybe, if we're doing this, we should look at a place that works for both of us."

"Where would that be?" he asked gently as if he knew there wasn't one. He could easily go anywhere, especially to be closer to his daughter and grandkid. Idaho was over a day's drive from my business and my family. Colt's found family in my brother and cousin were in Coal Haven, and there was little in Bismarck for Colt. He refused to admit he wouldn't be happy working inside all day and punching a time clock. He might not be too proud to take on any sort of work, but he loved ranching. I didn't want to be the one to take it away from him.

"Can we table the discussion for now? Until after Christmas?" A tiny spark of panic ignited in my chest. What if he wanted to move to Idaho? Could I leave my family and my business? I would, but shouldn't this decision be easier? Seven years we'd missed, and we were struggling in our first week. What if we weren't meant to be together?

"Yeah." He pressed a firm kiss to my lips. "We'll figure it out, okay?" He might not be able to read my mind, but my fraught expression must be transparent.

"Okay."

He tucked me into his side. The coolness from outside had been thoroughly chased away by his body heat, a warmth I was quickly becoming used to, going to sleep next to, and waking up beside.

We had to be able to figure our lives out. I didn't want

to get the best present of my life only to have to return him on December twenty-sixth.

* * *

Colt

The coffee shop buzzed around us. Ben had stayed at the ranch with Berkley, giving Brittany some time to hang out child-free. Nora was chatting with the owner about coffee roasts, blends, and flavors. Their words were a different language to me. When they delved into the specialty food items, I gestured for Brittany to take a seat. Nora was in her element and would be a while, and I'd like to watch her animated face and her sheer delight in discussing her passion.

Nora's brother and cousins had politely listened to her rattle on about various ingredients and substitutions. Eventually, the lack of interest had discouraged her, and she hadn't talked about her passion.

I had noticed her clam up, but it wasn't like I could slide next to her and ask about a decent egg substitute. I didn't have an egg allergy, for one. I didn't bake for another.

Watching her hands fly and see her excitedly nod as she geeked out with the baker and owner of the little shop we were in was a special treat.

If she moved to Coal Haven, she wouldn't have this. I'd been to her coffee place in Bismarck with Holden before. Her business only highlighted how out of my league she was.

I didn't care to keep falling short.

Brittany waggled her finger between me and Nora.

"However this happened, I'm glad it did. I like how you are with her."

Her approval meant everything. "How's that?"

"Settled."

I could only nod. Brittany had no idea how unsettled I was. "I've never gotten her a present." I peered into my mug of black coffee. What the hell was it called? Americana? I gave as little thought to the coffee I drank as I did to the women I'd dated before Nora. One cup and it'd be gone. Any more than that, and I was just asking for an uncomfortable day.

Was I ready to be drinking fancy roasts and waking to the sounds of city traffic drifting into the bedroom? For her? Hell, yeah. But being the reason behind my sudden change of living bugged her, and I didn't like the way it was tearing her up. She'd dump my ass so I could be free to go wherever I wanted.

Where I wanted to be was with her.

Fuck, we had to figure this out. The anxiety in Nora's eyes from yesterday morning gutted me. She worried we were doomed. The way we'd finally gotten together had ended us—or showed us why we hadn't crossed the divide earlier.

"What does she like?" Brittany asked, stopping me from riding circles around the problem.

"Those ugly sweaters." Every damn day, I looked forward to what she'd wear. When she lived with her mom after college, she had been more subdued around the holidays. I was glad she wasn't holding back around my family.

"They're cute." Brittany tipped her head as she inspected the shirt Nora wore today. A gaudy blue material with small ornaments sewn onto the front. Her leggings were a golden yellow. She looked like an elf that wandered out of the North Pole. "She makes them cute," Brittany amended.

I grunted my agreement. I'd take the yellow-brick-road leggings any day if it meant seeing the curve of her thighs. "She likes the challenge of baking for people with food allergies and sensitivities. I think she learned coffee as a vehicle to sell her food."

"That doesn't give us many ideas for presents. What else does she like? Hobbies?"

I didn't have to think about it. "She likes outdoor activities. She used to be a camp counselor. Loved working with kids."

"You gonna give her a baby for Christmas?" Brittany's tone was teasing, but my brain wanted to seriously shout *yes*.

A kid. The condo life and close neighbors would be worth having kids with Nora.

I could be a dad. I could do all the dad things I missed out on with Brittany.

How would I teach a kid to ride a horse in Bismarck? Drive a tractor? What if we had more than one child? Would they have to wait for the holidays when we visited other Barrons so they could go snowmobiling and four-wheeling like Nora and Holden had when they were younger?

"Wouldn't that be weird for you?" I asked, afraid she'd answer honestly.

"No. Why?" When she noticed my surprise, she shook her head. "All the best stuff is a little weird, Colt. I have a dad I didn't know until I was almost out of high school. Another dad I'm not biologically related to who I adore. A mom only fifteen years older than me. I have half-siblings and stepsiblings. Some might say my life is odd. To me, it's normal and perfect. What's a brother or sister who's thirty-ish years younger than me?"

I chuckled at the last bit, but my throat was growing thick. I had a good kid. A damn good kid.

"We have to figure out where we'll live first." I told Brittany about the job offer from Stetson. Definitely not something I would've confessed to my daughter before. I wouldn't have burdened her with any of it. But the interest and concern on her face wasn't regret I was sharing. She cared about me, and I had to let her in so she knew I loved her. Saying it wasn't good enough.

"Coal Haven has become your home, hasn't it?" she asked.

"How do you mean?"

"When I went to college in Denver, that place wasn't home. I lived there for four years." She gave me a pointed look. "You made that possible, but it was never more than the town I went to school in. It's why I moved back to Idaho Falls. It's home." She gestured around the shop with her coffee mug. "You have no compulsion to visit this town just to see me. It's like instinctively, you know there are too many people you'd run into who'd remember the old you. Too many memories. You stayed in Coal Haven for a reason." She took a sip of her mostly milk coffee drink and let her words sink in. "Or you would've left like you did everywhere else. Your life is there."

"I'm planning to move to be with Nora." And convincing her I was okay with it.

She shrugged. "From what you said, it's not far away. But it's okay to tell her what you want. You two are going to be a team."

What she said was true, but I wasn't overriding what Nora wanted with my superficial wishes. I'd made sure I had no ties for so long, I wasn't letting location hold me back. "We're going to figure it all out after Christmas. Until then, I need a present for her to open."

Brittany studied me until I started to squirm. She got that trait from her mother. Being held accountable was the main reason why I'd ditched my ex and everything else for years after. I was owning my decision now. That included moving.

"A bit at the last minute, isn't it, Colt?" Brittany finally asked with a hint of humor. A beat of relief hit me the heavy part of our conversation was done. "You're driving all day tomorrow to get back for Christmas Day."

"She took me by surprise." In so many ways.

Brittany's gaze flicked toward Nora. The deviousness that infused her brown eyes came from me. "She's coming. I'll take her to the bakery on the corner, and you do what you gotta do."

Eight

NORA

Colt and I were stashed in the little motel in Coal Haven. I was sprawled across the bed, relaxing after a tense drive. I hadn't even been behind the wheel. Once we'd crossed over the Montana border into North Dakota, a squall had kicked up, making the road almost impossible to see at times.

Colt had driven like it was clear as a bell and the middle of the day. I'd been crawling out of my seat, sure we were careening into a ditch any second.

I blew out a long breath. "That was stressful."

Out of the corner of my eye, he only lifted a shoulder as he spread out the food we'd ordered from Rattler's. Instead of the usual steak or pasta, Remington, one of the owners of the restaurant, had a Christmas Eve prime rib buffet with mashed potatoes and green bean casserole and the softest buns that would give me belly bloat until I looked six months pregnant. The kitchen had been closed when I called, but Remington had made us to-go boxes, refusing to let me get off the phone until I agreed to accept the food.

The rich, savory smells hit me. My taste buds watered. "You need to eat that bread before I'm tempted."

He picked up one, inspected it, and then took a big bite, looking me straight in the eye.

I groaned. "Is it as delicious as it looks?"

"Better."

I laughed and fell back onto the bed. "I knew it." I sighed. "Whoever my dad was, he passed on crappy genetics."

"You gonna eat or gush about my buns?"

"Your buns are gush-worthy, and I can sink my teeth into those."

He paused. "Keep talking like that, and the food is going to get cold while I devour you."

Grinning, I sat at the little round table across from him. We started eating. The meat was tender and delicious. The potatoes were savory yet fluffy like whipped cream. I ate the green beans, leaving as much of the casserole as I could. I didn't want to babysit the bathroom tonight. Colt knew a lot about me, but that part could wait.

With each bite, the quiet of the motel room sunk in. There was very little traffic outside, but nothing about this motel said Christmas or family. Colt and I were like two wanderers trying to find a place we both fit.

Coal Haven should've been the answer. Could it be? I had to get over myself. Let go of control of my coffee shop and...

"What's up?" Colt crushed his empty container and tossed it into the garbage.

"Just missing dessert." I didn't want to lie to him, but I also didn't want to talk about the unknowns in our future. He was willing to move in with me. I was willing to admit he wouldn't be happy. Content was different from happy, and I cared for him. More than I should admit to after less than a week together. He shouldn't have to sacrifice to be with me.

He got up and went to the bags Remington had packed our food in. Withdrawing another white container, he looked over his shoulder. "Just what would you do for some of Rattler's flourless cake?"

I sucked in a gasp. "You got some?"

"I know your sweet tooth, Nora. You wouldn't have been doing all those baking experiments if you liked salty food more than sweets."

I clapped my hands, the melancholy from earlier slipping off my shoulders. The uncertainty might be waiting in the wings, but I had a guy who delighted me with little surprises.

He placed the box in the middle of the table and brandished his fork. "Plan to tell me what's really wrong?"

I sighed. The downside of landing a really good guy was that he cared when something was bothering me. "It's nothing, really."

"Nora, you lie like shit. It's why you can't cheat at cards."

"I don't cheat at cards." Anymore.

"Not with that expressive face you don't."

I rolled my eyes and fought back a smile. "Once, when I was in college, and it shouldn't get held against me."

"Spill it." He snatched my fork from my hand. "And then you get the goodies."

I would eat this cake with my fingers, and he knew it. But I sat back, my shoulders drooped. "The motel is messing with me. I've always wanted a Christmas like what's on TV, you know. Big house decorated to the nines. Happy family to share the day."

He handed me the fork. "But you can't fit Holden and Emery and all their kids in your condo."

"No." My annoying neighbor would've made sure to tell me how loud everyone was. "The happy part ruled out having Christmas at Mom's."

He nodded and used my fork to cut off a giant piece. Then he held it up for me to take the bite.

I made sure to meet his gaze when I wrapped my lips around the utensil. To add extra naughtiness, I moaned. The dessert earned the sound, sweet and rich and full of sin, but the way his eyes darkened and he adjusted how he was sitting was even better.

"You're wicked."

Smiling around my mouthful, I cut another chunk off and finished chewing. "It's fine though. Really. I'm with you, and that's something I never thought I'd get." I smiled when I was rewarded with another blush.

When we finished the dessert, he got up. "I have to grab something out of the pickup."

"I'll jump in the shower before bed." After a long day of sitting so close to Colt and not being able to do anything about it, I had plans for when we crawled into bed. But first, I had to wash away the anxiety sweat from the treacherous last couple of hours on the road.

In the bathroom, I rushed through the shower. It was late, and we'd be up early. I didn't want to miss the frenzy of the kids opening their gifts, the homey and inviting warmth of Holden's house, and the beautiful chaos of his large family. He said Mom hadn't been invited. They'd planned for her to be out of town, and they wanted me and Colt there. As Holden said, *I'm gonna watch that fucker have to sit through an entire holiday without running off to hole himself up.*

Someday, I'd have that too. Someday, maybe I could

have it with Colt. I frowned as I toweled off. Did he want more kids? Would he think his age was a problem again? The fact that he was a grandparent? The gnawing worry was back in my gut. Good thing I hadn't eaten a lot of the green bean casserole.

When I stepped out of the bathroom, wrapped in a thin towel, the lights were off. A shimmery glow came from the dresser next to the TV. A two-foot-tall Christmas tree was decked out with lights, and small presents were piled underneath.

My damp hair dripped onto my bare shoulders, and the drop rolled into the towel. My Christmas pajamas with the large present on the shirt were in my luggage. Colt liked to claim he was unwrapping his gift when he took the top off, but I figured we'd go straight to no clothes first.

He had other plans. And he was on the phone. Had Brittany checked on him?

He glanced up to see me in nothing but a towel looking from him to the small tree. "Gotta go." He disconnected and set the device on the table.

"What's this?" As if I didn't know. A bloom of emotion grew larger in my chest. I loved this man. I'd fallen for him a long time ago, but anything I withheld out of self-preservation was annihilated. He'd planned ahead in Idaho Falls and bought Christmas decor for tonight. Presents too.

"Next time, the decorations will be wall to wall." His hair was windswept from his run out to the pickup. He'd shoved his hands in the pockets of his jeans and monitored my reaction.

Was he worried it wasn't enough?

I flew into his arms, my towel staying in place. "I can't believe you did this." I pulled away. "*When* did you do this?"

The tension drained out of him. "My daughter's a crafty one."

I let out a scandalized gasp. "You mean she wasn't just trying to bond with me?"

I grinned and looked at the little burst of Christmas in a plain motel room in my hometown. The house I grew up in, that I shouldn't feel so nostalgic toward, was mere miles away. Maybe it was empty. Maybe my mother, the Grinch, was roaming and grumping. Either way, I was done with it. A piece of my heart died with the idea that my childhood home could be a happy place, but the motel room was a fresh start. A blank slate that Colt had decorated just for me.

"Thank you."

"For you? Anything. Open a present."

I eyed the three neatly wrapped gifts. "The one I got for you is in my car." Which was parked at Holden's.

The corner of his mouth lifted. "My pocketknife can wait."

I chuckled. "How'd you know?"

I'd gotten him a pocketknife every year since the first Christmas he worked for Mom. I'd left it in front of his door each Christmas Eve. On Christmas Day, he'd be on his own while Mom and I crashed other family members' holiday parties. By the time I was out of college, he'd been invited to Stetson's or Holden's, or even one of my uncles' places. But I'd still put the pocketknife on his doorstep each Christmas Eve.

"Those gifts are one of the most constant things in my life."

Gah. My heart. "You used them, so I kept buying them."

He sobered. "Until I got to know Brittany, they were the only gift I got."

If we managed to traverse the next year and ended up in

the same spot next Christmas, he was getting loads of gifts. I gave him a quick kiss. Anything longer and my towel would come off, and gifts wouldn't get opened. I grabbed the larger rectangular present.

"Good choice," he said and sat on the edge of the bed.

I opened the green wrapping with small candy canes.

"I didn't wrap them," he said like it was a confession. I knew he hadn't. He was good at a lot of things, but perfectly centered tiny creases weren't it. "It would've been covered in tape and ruined the surprise."

"You didn't have to get me anything, you know."

"I was gonna put a bow on my dick, but I didn't think that was enough."

Laughing, I bared a clothing box. Inside was the most charming yet most horrendous Christmas sweater I'd ever seen. I held it up. Glitter fell into the tissue paper that the garment had been wrapped in. The main fabric was gold, same as the glitter tree ornament on the front. The only non-gold color was the green fringe that made up the tree around the obnoxious gold ornaments. "It's perfect. So perfect I can't even wear it tomorrow, or Emery will gut me for leaving a trail of glitter in the house. But I might wear it anyway."

His blush was back. I'd never get tired of seeing it. "It hung in the window like it was waiting for you."

I carefully folded the fabric glitter bomb into the box and selected the second gift. I unwrapped the narrow rectangular box. Inside was a slender piece of metal decorated with horseshoes and roses. A beautiful pocketknife. "Colt."

"You kept buying them for me, but don't think I didn't notice you never had one."

"Because I could always ask to use yours." And get a thrill out of seeing him brandish a gift I'd gotten him. I ran my finger along the cool metal. "It's gorgeous. I'm almost afraid to use it."

"Don't you dare waste a nice tool." He jutted his chin to the small but mighty tree.

One more gift waited for me. The box was smaller, square, and heavier. Strangely heavy for such a small box. I removed the wrapping and opened the top of the white box. On a pad of white foam was a silver horseshoe. *Welcome* was along the curve of the shoe.

"We're going to hang it in our place." He wrapped an arm around me, his hand landing at my hip. "Wherever you are is where I am, and I don't care where on this earth it is. As long as you're there."

The backs of my eyes burned. I didn't deserve him. I was too much like my mother. Selfish, stubborn, and scared. Mom feared her feelings, and I was just as scared of failing as Colt. When I brushed off the idea of opening a second store, I assumed lightning struck once. Mom's words stained my view of my success, but the truth was, I could've pumped my trust fund into the coffee shop and failed. But I'd planned and went to school for business. I succeeded.

I leaned my head into his chest. All the emotions inside me pressed against my rib cage until my heart burst out of my chest. This man was special. He treated me better than any ex, and it'd been mere days since we crossed the line to a couple. He stood up for me. He was sacrificing for me.

What would I do for him? For us?

As soon as I saw the tree and the gifts, I knew I'd give up my condo and move to Coal Haven. My decision was made. "Colt. Take that job with Stetson."

"But—"

"I can open a second shop. In Coal Haven." I kissed his neck, the short strands of his beard tickling my face. "We'll build. I'll learn to ignore Mom and enjoy being closer to my family."

"A second shop? You said you didn't think you could split between more than one."

Sudden shyness struck me, as it often did when talking about my business. I was five years in and going strong. Business was booming and growing. "Years ago, I did an analysis of the area. Then I had a fight with Mom and decided it'd never work. But I'm tired of letting her, and to some extent my uncles, influence what I do. You're willing to walk away from them. I'm willing to live among them. No coffee shop has opened yet, and I think the economy around here has only gotten stronger. Smaller populations have supported coffee shops—"

He put his fingers on my lips. "If you're trying to justify your decision, you have to know I support you one hundred percent. I knew your first attempt was going to kick ass. Your second one will kick even more butt."

His confidence was unwavering. All the support I could ever want. I pushed him back and crawled on top of him. He spread his arms out like he was a willing sacrifice to the impossible swell of emotions I had to release. "How can you be so supportive?"

"You're a Barron for one. They get what they want. And look what you did with the farmers' market."

I had also walked into a solid foundation thanks to my cousin Isla. Yet Colt was unfailingly resolute in his confidence in me. "Colt, I know your secret."

He cocked a brow.

"You're sweet."

"Only with you, snow angel." He planted his big hands on my bare thighs. "Everyone else can fuck off."

I started unbuttoning his shirt. "Are you going to take that job with Stetson?"

"Are you sure you want to move back?" His hands flexed over my skin. He needed reassurance.

"This is your home. My home. We'd be happier here, nosy family and townsfolk and all." I leaned down, unintentionally grinding into his already solid erection behind the fly of his jeans. Pleasure shot through my core. "We are going to be the center of gossip for *weeks*."

"I'm ready if you are." Sincerity spilled from his expression. "I'm ready for a lot."

My breath caught. I'd find out what he meant later. We had time, and I had to make sure he knew I was serious. "So, you're going to tell Stetson you'll work for him?"

"Baby, you're sitting on my dick. I'm gonna do whatever you say."

"Good. And we'll stay…" I looked around the square motel room. "Here. Or at the condo. Until we find a house." I ripped his shirt open and growled. His undershirt was in the way. "You are entirely overdressed."

"Funny, I was thinking the same about you." He tugged the notch holding my towel closed free. Shivers erupted over my skin as the fabric slid off me. He palmed my breasts. I ground into him. The clasp of his pants dug into me, but the hard ridge under his jeans notched perfectly into my seam.

"Colt," I whined.

"I got you." He flicked a finger through my wetness, and I hissed, rocking into him.

I narrowed my world onto him, blocking everything else out. This motel room was a fresh start. It was almost midnight, and I would ring in my favorite holiday deliriously orgasmic.

He flipped open his jeans. Our fingers tangled as I rushed to free his impressive erection. I'd never get tired of being surprised and overwhelmed by his size. I loved the way his veins traced up and down his shaft. Strength radiated through him, head to toe, and he kept it all perfectly leashed until he thought it was necessary. Tonight, he would use his skills for pure pleasure.

He was digging in his back pocket for a condom. I eased up only so he could sheath himself, and then I was sinking on him, a ragged moan leaving my body.

"I love the way you fill me."

"You're perfect, Nora." He rolled up, cradling me to him to keep me from slipping off his lap.

I rode him, and he sucked and licked at my nipples. Wrapping his head in my embrace, I let shivers track up and down my spine at the sensation of his lips, his tongue, and his beard. Beard burn was becoming my favorite body decoration.

"*Yes*, Colt."

His fingers dug into my ass. I kept going, letting the energy spark between us until a wildfire roared. My body was flushed, and we were both breathing heavily. I was almost there, and like he sensed how close I was and that all I needed was a little shove, he wedged his hand between us and stroked my clit.

I should've slid right off his lap. His ass was on the edge of the bed. We should both be on the floor, but he held us in place. He had me. He always would.

I catapulted off the edge. I let out one cry before biting my lip to keep any other guests from hearing what we were doing. He went taut, his hips thrusting up in short strokes, coming, but he tilted his head back. I claimed his mouth, using him to keep quiet like he intended me to.

Aftershocks of pleasure rippled through me. His hold eased, but he didn't move me off right away. I broke away and looked into his dark eyes. A pensive energy circled his irises. I brushed a thumb along the corner of his eye.

His gaze flickered. "I almost didn't get a condom in time."

"Was I too much?"

"No, baby, you're never too much. I didn't want anything between us."

"Me either." But I wasn't on birth control. He didn't have to say that he didn't want kids. I wouldn't take it personally. His past complicated the issue, and our relationship was so new.

"And I..." He worked his jaw back and forth. "And I thought I'd really like to see my kid growing in your belly."

Surprise. Lust. Excitement. They all swirled inside me. His gaze didn't dip. He wasn't lying. He wasn't telling me something he thought I wanted to hear. Something I dreamed of hearing from him.

"You want more kids?"

"I never thought I would. But around you?" He let out a puff of air. "When I held Berkley, I couldn't help but wonder if I could do it. Then Brittany told me she'd be thrilled."

I ran my thumb down the line of shock between his brows. "You put your assumptions in her head."

"My grandkid would be older than her aunt or uncle. It'd be an issue." The corner of his mouth kicked up. "Not for her. And if it's not for you, then I'm on board. I know how much you want kids," he finished quietly.

This thing between us was new, but we hit the ground running. We'd wasted enough time. "I want a house full of laughter. I want to help our kids with 4-H animals. Go to school performances with a smile." Mom had grumbled the whole way and missed half of them. "I want to make a big deal out of birthdays and holidays and get excited when they tell me their plans for their future." I cupped his face. "But mostly, I want a dad who'll be invested. So if we're going to do this, it has to be something you're sure of. I know how significant having a kid would be for you."

"I want kids with you." He wrapped his hand around the back of my neck and rolled us to the side. "Let me get rid of this condom and fuck it—we can start trying tonight."

* * *

Colt

Wrapping paper littered the floor of Holden's living room. I had my brand-new pocketknife in the back pocket of my jeans. The tool was small with an inscription that said *It's not the size that matters but being in the right place at the right time.*

Holden had laughed his merry little ass off.

His kids lounged around. The teens were playing on their phones. The youngest were building Legos, an activity I never had the patience for. Nora had stocked them all up on Legos, even the oldest, who was going to college soon.

Fuck, had that much time passed? The kid hadn't been a teen when Holden and Emery met. Nora had helped take Emery's kids horseback riding. I'd been out that day, too, and I'd barely been able to concentrate while watching Nora with the kids.

I'd been stuck in a cycle of Groundhog Day since then, like I'd been afraid of fucking up more. Until a bombshell with a penchant for clean eating found me naked in her mom's kitchen.

Yeah, maybe we wouldn't tell anyone about that.

Nora was on the floor with her niece and nephew. She'd already been out sledding while Holden and I bullshitted, mostly about what the hell his mom was going to do with the ranch. His grin told me he wasn't upset. He rather liked seeing his mom in a predicament.

I'd texted Stetson back, asking him when he wanted me to start. Different Barron, same work. The pressure in my chest eased. I didn't dream of a ranch of my own. With the Barrons, I was part of a legacy, and that was enough for me.

Stetson said I could show up the day after the new year began. I was getting a proper vacation whether I liked it or not. I'd use the week to find a place to rent and help Nora move.

I looked around the house, full of hors d'œuvre trays sitting out to get picked on throughout the day, half-eaten pies on the island, and kids lounging in every chair and on the couch and floor.

Was I ready for this level of chaos?

The resounding answer was yes. About damn time.

I'd missed a lot with my daughter, and I'd never shed that sense of loss. But I was done restricting myself from ever having a chance at it again.

The right woman changed everything.

First, I had changed myself.

My phone buzzed. I checked it while Holden and Emery talked about leftover recipes. I used to stuff envy away when I witnessed them being a normal couple, but now I pictured Nora talking about her ideas for leftovers next year and I couldn't fucking wait. Non-dairy, non-gluten ideas and all.

The message said **Ready**.

I got up and squatted next to Nora. "Mind if we go?"

It was evening, but not terribly late. She peeked at the clock on the wall. "Oh, it's that late already. Yes, it's almost Grady's bedtime."

"I don't have to go to bed early." He blinked his big eyes at his parents. "It's Christmas."

"Another hour, bud," Holden said as he met us at the

door on the tail of Grady's protests. "Thanks for coming." He did the side hug to Nora, squeezing her tight. "Kind of excited to have you back in town again."

He turned to me. His gaze was assessing. "Still feels weird, I'm not gonna lie."

I shrugged. "Get used to it."

He grinned. "Now it feels real."

It took another ten minutes to get out the door. Nora had gotten three different hugs from the kids until Holden shooed us out before Grady incorporated us into the bedtime routine.

"We can get your car in the morning," I told her and loaded her in the pickup. Leaving it at Holden's one more day wouldn't hurt, and Nora needed to ride with me. We had a stop to make, and I hoped like hell I wouldn't regret it.

The churn in my gut said I might.

Nora frowned at me. I gave her a hard time for her attempt at cheating at cards, but I was a shit liar too. "Is something wrong?" she asked.

"I hope not." I pulled out of Holden's place, thankful Kira's house was only a minute away. I turned into the yard.

"Did you forget something?" She squinted at the big piney wreath gracing the front door of the house. "That's a first." When I parked by the side door, she blinked at me. "Colt."

Her flat tone was full of warning. I didn't want to trick her, but I also wanted what was best for her. The only problem was that I wasn't in control of what happened next. "Look, I can't promise we're not walking into a shit show. All I'm saying is give her a chance, and as soon as you want to leave, I'll burn rubber on the way out."

She narrowed her eyes. "Did you two plan something?"

I shook my head. "I think us leaving bothered her more

than she could've imagined." I met Nora's gaze. "I think it terrified her."

I'd never heard Kira so distraught. The woman seemed like the emotional equivalent of a stone, but she wasn't a rock, and most of us forgot that. She had a helluva shell, thick with a million coats of hurt feelings and lost opportunities, but it was still a shell. She was a complicated person like the rest of us.

Or I could be fucking wrong, and I risked Nora's Christmas on it.

Indecision played over Nora's pretty features. Her mouth was set as she glanced from me to the house.

"She gets one minute, and then we're gone," she finally said.

"Got it."

Nine

NORA

I didn't go to the side door. Snow crunched under my boots as I went to the front door and rang the doorbell like a proper guest. I wasn't wearing my new glitter bomb sweater, but I had on a Christmas sweater underneath my winter coat. My niece Afton said the green reminded her of vomit, and I said I'd re-gift it to her for next year. I wouldn't have changed if I'd known I was seeing Mom, but I didn't care to defend my choice of looks on Christmas Day. My red plaid leggings would irritate her enough.

I faced the front door. Did the doorbell even work?

The door creaked open to Mom. She looked as stiff as I felt but with a fresh tan and sun-bleached streaks in her hair. Instead of her standard heather-gray Barron Ranch hoodie, she wore a beige sweater with green and red balls of decoration hanging on the hem. The front said *This is my ugly Christmas sweater.*

Had her luggage gotten lost? Did she have nothing else to wear? Had a body snatcher replaced my mom and would they be less cranky?

"You came." Her tone was frank, but the tremor of surprise was audible.

"Yes, Colt said—" I leaned to the side, unable to believe the festive clutter I was seeing. "What happened here?"

Behind Mom was a living room that a Christmas clearance sale threw up in. A tree that tilted to the side and should have toppled over already thanks to the several pounds of decorations hanging on it was sitting in front of the picture window. So many strings of lights were wrapped around the poor thing, it looked like a mob hit that should get dumped in the river, but it lit up the room as bright as an airport runway.

Mom ran her tongue across her teeth. "Colt said you always wanted the house done up for Christmas."

When did he tell her that? Then I leaned over again, movement catching my eye. "Is that a train set?"

"Don't they do that shit?" Mom cleared her throat. "I mean, don't people decorate with trains around the tree?"

"I...don't know." I reached behind me, needing a stabilizing force. My childhood home never looked this bright and cheerful nor this messy. Mom hated busyness in her surroundings. Colt closed his big warm hand around mine, anchoring me. "You did this?"

"For you." She stepped back and opened the door further. "You might as well come in and see all of it."

For me? I had to have heard her wrong. The older I got, the less Mom had done for me. But the decorations couldn't be denied. They weren't there when I packed my stuff, and Coal Haven wasn't known to have Santa's elves with poor taste in decor who broke into houses.

Colt gave my hand a reassuring squeeze. I stepped in, and his heat was a wall behind me. The old farmhouse had a shallow entry, and we were basically in the main room.

I could see the entirety of her decoration attempts. "Oh my..."

Mom didn't possess one ounce of interior design knowledge, and it showed clearer than a neon sign at the bar. Paper bells were taped to the ceiling. Gold-and-silver garland smothered the fireplace and was strung along the back of the furniture. Strings of lights rounded the window. Half weren't lit, and part of the length had come loose to hang to the floor.

"Where did you get all this?" I asked, not going any farther inside.

"All the stores were closed, so I made a few calls." She propped her hands on her narrow hips. "Look, I know I was never cut out to be a mother—"

"You didn't even try." I faced her directly. She wasn't off the hook after a cluttered attempt to be festive. "How would you even know?"

"You just know, Nora." She said it so simply I wasn't sure if I should be offended or not.

"Okay. But you can at least be civil to me even if you never wanted me."

"Civil never got me nowhere." When I took a step toward the door, Mom held her hands up. "I'm not making excuses. I am the way I am, and it's not a good fit with kind-hearted people like you. But you're my family. Honest to God, last night it finally sunk in that you and Colt treat me better than anyone else in my life. Holden too, of course. Both of you kids managed to be the best thing I ever did, and I don't know how that happened." She gestured toward Colt. "Even he was an impulse hire. The first guy not to assume I didn't know a damn thing—even after he helped me with that ornery bastard of a horse."

"What are you saying?" I asked, unsure what her goal was. Temptation to be happy tiptoed through me, but I couldn't give in. This was my mother.

Her hard gaze dropped to the floor. "Colt's damn lucky to get you." She pursed her lips like she wasn't sure if she should keep talking. "I knew as soon as he found someone, he was gone."

Mom was making a lot of confessions I never expected her to utter, but I wasn't letting her off easy. "You didn't know that. You assumed, and you didn't give him enough money to leave. That's pretty shitty."

Her jaw set again. "He was content until you told him not to be."

"So, it's my fault?"

"Alright, then," Colt said and tugged me toward the door. "I warned you, Kira."

"Shit, wait." She took a step toward us. "Yeah, I know I should've paid you better, Colt. What I'm saying is you never said otherwise, and I let that convince me there was nothing wrong with it. I don't like change."

"Not many do," he said, understanding her better than I did. "I was stuck in a rut too. But I'm not anymore. You gave me a chance to be a better man, Kira. And this is what happens when I decide to do something about it. I fell in love with your daughter, and I want to spend every day of my life with her."

I met his gaze, a cluster of fireworks lighting off around my heart. Colt Jensen just said he fell in love with me. He wasn't the type to show his feelings, but he said it, and he said it in front of Mom.

"I love you too." If he could be bold, so could I. I was a

Barron after all. Happiness gleamed in his eyes. I'd have to tell him as often as possible.

Mom studied us like she was trying to determine if we were real or trying to get under her skin. She was a naturally jaded person, and I couldn't take it personally. But I loved Colt. I'd been in love with him for a long time. I wasn't trying to fool anyone.

"I want you both to stay," she finally said.

"Both?" I asked. Did that mean she accepted our relationship?

"Colt can work for me. We can talk wages." She crossed her arms, her mouth set in its familiar stubborn line. "I'm keen on retirement anyway."

"Retire? You?" I couldn't picture Mom not ranching. She lived and breathed outdoor work. This was her empire to control. She could ignore Uncle Cameron when it came to her ranch.

She ducked her head. "I'll never quit, but I'd like to quit having to, know what I mean?"

I nodded. Being a business owner opened my eyes to the toil of turning a hobby into income and then having to support others. I was startled in the ways we were similar.

"You can do what Holden did," she said. "Pick out a plot of my land and build. It'll be yours."

"You want to *give* me part of your land?" She'd only ever talked about passing the land and ranch to Holden. "On what condition?"

"No condition." She lifted her chin, respectful challenge in her eyes. "You were so damn determined to be different from me, but I think we're more alike than you care to admit. This place is in your blood, and you hate living in the city."

"I don't *hate* it," I mumbled, but she gave me a knowing look. "Fine, that's why I came home while you were gone. I needed some open space and to hear the cows and pet some horses."

"That fancy coffee shop of yours doesn't have mooing?" She held her hand up for the third time. "I'm still me. I'm gonna give my daughter shit for her fancy drinks and her dainty food."

A smile teased my lips, but I wasn't satisfied. "Can you at least acknowledge that some foods make me sick, and that's why I eat differently than you?"

"I can do that. I ain't eating it though."

I arched a brow. "Bet you had all the fancy dishes at the beach resort."

"For those prices, you're damn right I ate everything they included in the package."

I chuckled, and Mom smiled, a genuine grin that wasn't soothing an intentional barb. She was my mother. I might not get traditional motherly love, but we could still have a relationship that was uniquely us.

I faced Colt. His expression was carefully neutral, as it often was around Mom. "We have some things to talk about."

He dipped his head. "I took a job with Stetson," he said to Mom.

"I know." She smacked her lips. "He probably offered it only because he knew it'd chap my ass." She rolled her shoulders. "And it did."

I could see Stetson doing that. I might be more like Mom than I thought—and Stetson had a lot of his dad in him.

"I'd like to open a second coffee shop in town."

She appraised me. "Figured you would. Cameron and Naomi have been discouraging others, hoping you'd bring your business here."

Shock hit me square in the chest. Why would my family

deprive others so I could have an advantage? But that was the way of my mom and uncles. It was hard not to appreciate their almost toxic loyalty—and be even more grateful my brother, cousins, and I were different.

"I'll talk to Stetson," Colt said. "If he needs help..."

"He don't," Mom said. "Cameron's retiring, and then Stetson will wish he didn't have help. Besides, if you and Nora are going to be getting the ranch—"

"What?" The constant surprises were making me dizzy. I gave my head a small shake. First the land, and now the ranch?

"I never said I wouldn't pass a part of the ranch down to you." The gotcha look in her eye was all Mom. But sincere happiness crowded in. "Nora, you weren't ever set on just ranching, and I didn't want you to sell your portion off."

"I wouldn't have." Would I?

"Hired someone else to manage it," she added.

That I would've had to do.

"I couldn't guarantee Colt would stick around when I was gone." She waved at the two of us. "But this changes things. It's...it feels right."

I could be insulted that Colt was the clincher, but she was right. Colt took pride in his work, he strove to do a good job, but he cared about this place, the land, and the animals. I couldn't imagine being on this ranch without him.

"Wait." Colt tucked me into him. "What are you saying?"

Mom's lips twitched. Did she enjoy shocking Colt? "I'm saying you're family, Colt, whether you like it or not. I'm saying I've already talked to Holden about what Nora gets, and if you're making her an honest woman after shacking up all week, then this place will be yours too. Give me five years. Maybe three. The sand on the beach was perfect this year." She pressed her hands into her hips again. "I know you ate at Holden's, but I have some bars." She flicked her gaze to meet Colt's. "Flourless, dairy-free bars."

"Did you bake?" How many more shocks was I getting tonight? Mom didn't bake traditional desserts. She didn't bake at all.

"God, no. None of us want that. I owe your aunt Willow a ton after all this though," she grumbled.

My uncle Bruce's wife was as sweet as they come, and she'd never call in the favor. She'd be happy Mom finally came crawling to her and had to be nice to get some help.

Mom stuffed her hands in the back pockets of her jeans. "You two can stay in the apartment. It's yours as long as you need it."

"Appreciate it," Colt said roughly. His brows were drawn. The news would take a while for him to digest. He might never feel worthy, but he'd likely spend every day of his life proving he was.

"Okay." She gave a firm nod. "Okay. I, uh, I'll go get the dessert."

She disappeared into the kitchen where I first saw Colt in the buff.

I spun into him. "What the hell just happened? How? When?"

His stunned gaze was on the kitchen. "The phone call last night. I told her if she wanted to make amends, she'd have to show you that she cared about you and what you wanted in life."

Then he'd kept it to himself in case she decided I wasn't worth the trouble.

I faced the loud living room. She must've spent all night and day getting supplies and decorating. The tree even tilted in the same direction as the tree she'd thrown out.

"What's going on in that sharp mind of yours?" he murmured in my ear, nuzzling the lobe.

"How life-changing one power outage can be." I kissed him, withdrawing before I crawled up his body in my mom's entryway.

He steered me toward the kitchen. "You think it was the power outage or finding me naked?"

Epilogue

NORA

Our new house was decorated to the nines. An eight-foot-tall tree was in the corner of the main living room with the huge windows that overlooked my favorite valley on our family land. The landscape was covered in snow and dotted with cattle, and I never tired of drinking my morning coffee and eating my chia pudding while staring at the view.

That I could do it on Christmas, with lights and garland and the train set Mom used last year puttering around the tree was pretty damn special.

Colt came up behind me and slid an arm around my waist. Our little three-month-old was tucked into the crook of his other arm.

"How's Kasey doing?" We'd named our son after Colt's mom. I never met the woman, but I knew he'd never quit regretting that he failed her by being a delinquent teen and a law-breaking adult. Kasey was helping him ease his guilt.

"He's good," Colt said, gently bouncing our little guy. "I was afraid those lungs of his would wake our guests."

Brittany, Ben, and Berkley were still sleeping in the basement guest room. She claimed it was quite healing to see how much he'd changed in the last year. When she was born and while she was growing up, he'd been in a bad place mentally and physically. But he was now a present father with her and Kasey and a doting grandfather.

She made him start decreasing the amount of money he sent to Berkley. They settled on an amount, and he'd started an account for Kasey.

When we built, we'd made sure there were enough guest rooms for them and also extra bedrooms in case we had more kids.

We were planning for another, but I needed time to adjust after birthing Colt's big baby. Kasey had stubbornly sat on my bladder and refused to move for months. After he was born, he wouldn't sleep at night and had a permanent cranky expression that gave me the giggles. I just knew he was going to be a lot like my mom.

I used a spoonful of chia pudding to gesture to the window. "I'll never get tired of this view or this house."

Colt didn't blanch when he caught me eating chia pudding anymore, but he gave me a *you know I'm not eating that* look.

I grinned and stuffed the spoon in my mouth. "I think I'll debut this flavor at the Coal Haven shop first."

"You should do both. You know it'll be a hit."

I did. Several other flavors of my chia pudding were sold out regularly, and I was starting on seasonal flavors. This was a red velvet concoction that would pair well with Valentine's Day.

But first, I got to celebrate my first time hosting a big Christmas. I promised my mom and brother I'd have "regular" food in addition to Nora-gut-friendly food. Brittany enjoyed my various concoctions, and she even had a standing order for a shipment of gluten-free muffins each month to go with her coffee. I gave her the family discount of free.

"I'm gonna do chores." Colt pressed the blanket beneath Kasey's chin. "Need me to do anything before I go?"

"No, everything's ready to throw in the oven."

Mom had been right about Stetson. He could've used the help, and Colt would continue lending a hand like he'd always had before, but with Uncle Cameron's impending retirement, he'd be fine. Aunt Naomi was working less and spending more time with her grandkids too.

I couldn't believe how life had changed so much since growing up. The last year came at warp speed. The house was done at the end of the summer. My second coffee shop opened in the fall. And my number one customer was my mom.

Turned out she was a closet gourmet coffee aficionado. She had another beach vacation scheduled this year with the same guy from last year, but she waited until after Christmas to go. She'd be here soon. To no one's surprise, she got along with Brittany. The girl had too much of Colt's personality for them not to like each other.

Colt pressed his mouth against mine, his hand sliding down my ass. "You know what we should fit in while everyone's sleeping?"

"Won't you be late for chores?" I knew damn well he'd be late for anything for sex.

"Baby, I'm old. I won't take long."

I laughed and smothered my mouth with my fingers to keep from waking the baby. The guy had stamina to spare.

He went up the stairs, and I followed. Before he disappeared into the nursery, he stopped and pinned me with a hot gaze. I was wearing my pajama top with the large, wrapped gift on the front. "Don't you dare take those pajamas off. I get to unwrap my present."

I trailed him into the nursery. Watching this big man who'd kept to himself for so long lay down a tiny baby with the utmost care, his expression full of love and a perpetual astonishment, never got old.

He always checked in with me before he went to work for the day. *Need me to do anything?*

My answer was the same as earlier. No. I had all I needed, and I meant it in so many ways.

———

Thank for reading! The Oil Barrons series might be done, but all the Barrons will eventually get their stories. Starting with the first book in my new series Oil Knights.

Once upon a time, Aggie Knight was a runaway bride, shattered thanks to the man she loved. Ten years later, she's now her ex's boss and her pieced together heart is holding firm. It has to. But seeing Ansen Barron every day will either put her back together, or finish tearing her apart. Find Aggie and Ansen's in A Reckless Memory.

For all the latest news, sneak peeks, free bonus content sign up for my newsletter.

Marie Johnston writes paranormal and contemporary romance and has collected several awards in both genres. Before she was a writer, she was a microbiologist. Depending on the situation, she can be oddly unconcerned about germs or weirdly phobic. She's also a licensed medical technician and has worked as a public health microbiologist and as a lab tech in hospital and clinic labs. Marie's been a volunteer EMT, a college instructor, a security guard, a phlebotomist, a hotel clerk, and a coffee pourer in a bingo hall. All fodder for a writer!! She has four kids, cats, and a half blind Corgie.

mariejohnstonwriter.com

Follow me:

* 9 7 8 1 9 5 1 0 6 7 7 8 6 *